## Praise for

A delightful romp into the immerses the reader in another time and place — 1946 in Southern California. We learn the slang, the music and the customs as we live the tension with Tom and Olivia. A pepper of humor, the sweetness of an old-fashioned love story and tense moments as detective and criminals bump heads make this an entertaining and memorable book.

~Coffeetime Romances~

*Initials for Murder* is a picture perfect snapshot of a "Dick Tracy" kind of story, complete with glamour, a puzzling mystery and a pretty lady who's stumbled onto something dangerous. It is a tried and true formula for a great story. **Venita Louise** is dead on the money with her descriptive scenes, mannerisms, and even her fashion sense, giving readers a peek in to the past. *Initials for Murder* is a well-crafted story with a twist on the ending.

~Fallen Angels Review~

# Mixed Nuts

## Venita Louise

Vintage Romance Publishing

Goose Creek, South Carolina

www.vrpublishing.com

# Mixed Nuts

Copyright ©2005 Venita Bart

Cover illustration copyright © 2005 by Patricia Foltz

Printed and bound in the United States of America. All rights reserved. No part of this book may be reproduced or transmitted in any form or by any means, electronic or mechanical, including photocopying, recording, or by an information storage and retrieval system-except by a reviewer who may quote brief passages in a review to be printed in a magazine, newspaper, or on the Web-without permission in writing from the publisher. For information, please contact Vintage Romance Publishing, LLC, 107 Clearview Circle , Goose Creek, SC 29445.

All characters in this book have no existence outside the imagination of the author and have no relation whatsoever to anyone bearing the same name or names save actual historical individuals. They are not even distantly inspired by any individual known or unknown to the author, and all incidents are pure invention.

ISBN: 0-9770107-6-7

PUBLISHED BY VINTAGE ROMANCE PUBLISHING, LLC

www.vrpublishing.com

*For my son, Joel.*

*My inspiration. My teacher. My light.*

# Chapter One

A slender ray of morning sunlight fell across the polished top of Frank Beal's Sherman Clay upright piano. He lightly tapped the keys with the tips of his fingers patiently waiting for inspiration to ignite.

"Good morning dad," greeted Matt, still nibbling on a wedge of toast.

Frank turned on the piano stool. "Morning Matt. Ready for school?"

Matt bounced in, his eight-year-old freckled face sparkling with a soap clean smile.

"Knock, knock," he said fairly squirming with anticipation.

Frank looked at his son. "What?"

"Knock, knock," Matt repeated.

Frank sighed and took his fingers off the keyboard. "All right," he said. "Who's there?"

Matt covered his mouth to muffle a giggle. "Little ole lady."

"Little ole lady who?" Frank asked trying to guess the puzzle.

"I didn't know you could yodel," Matt said throwing his head back to howl with laughter.

"Matt!" Joan called. "We have to go."

"Okay mom," he said as he rolled his big blue-green eyes.

Frank reached out to ruffle his son's hair.

Joan entered the room with her keys in hand. "The Roberts are getting a new Ford Fairlane station wagon this week-end." She placed a brochure on the piano in front of Frank. "What do you say we go to the Ford dealer tonight and have a look at them?"

Frank frowned. "What's wrong with our Caballero? Wouldn't you really rather have a Buick?"

"What?" She pulled her fox jacket on. "You want me to drive around in a seven year old car?" She shook her head. "I couldn't live with myself if I had to drive past their new car everyday."

"But I'm living with you," Frank replied.

"Exactly," Joan said as she turned toward the bottom of the stairs. "Melinda!" she called.

Objection marked Frank's face. "Honey, it's been a tough year. I'm really struggling with this new ad campaign and ideas aren't exactly flowing out of me." He stood up to walk toward her. "I think we should keep the spending down for awhile."

Joan smiled at him sweetly and tilted her head. "You've never let us down before." She stepped in front of him and wrapped her arms around his neck. She rose on tiptoe and planted a long wet one on him.

"Groady!" Matt grimaced.

Frank laughed and stepped over to playfully lift Matt up off his feet.

Clomping equal to the sound of horse hooves descended the stairs. "I'm ready," Melinda announced.

"You've something under your eyes," Joan said wetting her thumb and leaning toward her.

"Don't you dare wipe off my tweaks, Mother!" Melinda shrieked.

Joan's face pinched up. "Why do you need to wear tweaks?"

"Twiggy wears them; they make your eyes look bigger." Melinda widened her eyes then batted her false eyelashes and ran her fingers through her long blond hair.

"They look more like dangling caterpillars, and Twiggy gets paid to wear them," Joan snapped.

Melinda flicked her hair back and with half lidded eyes said, "I've decided to become a model, Mother."

"Where's your sister?" Joan asked as she adjusted her jacket.

Melinda shrugged and clomped to the front door. "I'm riding to school with Bobby today."

Joan turned toward her. "You've been seeing an awful lot of him lately."

Melinda grinned from ear to ear. "I know." She opened the door and stepped out.

"Wait! You're not going to wear those raggedy bell bottoms to school are you?"

The door closed.

"Frank, you need to talk to her," Joan said as she stepped up on the bottom stair. "Susan!" she called up.

Frank gave her a confused look. "Me?"

"You're her father aren't you? She's nearly sixteen."

"I always thought you would talk to the girls, and I would talk to Matt." He slinked an arm around Matt's shoulders. Matt beamed up at him.

Joan stepped down from the stair walking toward him. Frank returned to the piano and plopped back down on the stool.

"Since we have two girls and one boy, I guess that means I'm doing double duty. Do you think that's fair?" Joan asked.

Just then Susan bounced down the stairs. Frank released a breath.

"Good morning." She carried a clipboard and wore safety yellow hardhat. "I have made a thorough inspection of the house," she said solemnly, "and have found several safety violations." She tore a sheet from her clipboard and handed it to Frank. "You'll have to make these repairs before the end of the month, Daddy, or I will be forced to report you."

"You wouldn't," he said half smiling at her.

"Daddy," she said authoritatively. "You are in violation of official fire codes, and if you don't get them fixed I'll have to report you to the fire department."

He gazed absently at the paper.

"It's my civic duty, Daddy. Besides, you don't want your family and home to be at risk of death and destruction do you?"

"Noooo," Frank said slowly shook his head.

"Have you ever seen a dead body, Daddy?" She continued brightly. "We saw pictures in biology class. Did you know there is a substance called adipocere that forms over the fatty tissue after death?"

"Yuck!" Matt said and scrunched up his face.

"Commonly known as grave wax," Frank lisped and

turning his hands into claws, got off the bench and moved toward them dragging a leg behind him as he growled. Susan and Matt screamed and ran for the door.

"See you tonight," Joan said and kissed his cheek. "Don't forget we're going to the Ford dealer."

"You know honey, our Buick is just fine with me. It's roomy, dependable and still in style," he argued.

Joan bit back a grin then brushed her lips to his ear. "True but I can't help but think that a Ford is a better idea."

Frank watched silently as they crowded out the front door. He plopped down on the piano bench and studied his reflection in the glossy wood finish. A new piano would be nice, he thought. It could be just the thing to break this creative block. How about a baby grand? Or maybe just a padded bench? That would be nice, too. He wouldn't be able to afford that *and* a new Ford Fairlane. He began to play a lilting version of '*Moonlight Becomes You*'.

He rolled his hazel eyes to the ceiling. "*Grave wax becomes you*," he began to sing. "*It flows from your eyes. It certainly draws a mixture of flies*."

The doorbell rang. "Now what?" he said to himself. He stood. "I'm never going to get this ad finished with all these interruptions."

He walked over and opened the door and found himself staring at a hand holding up a rather large snail.

"Meester Beal, is thees jore snail?" It was the Robert's gardener, Tito Tortuga.

"I've never seen it before," Frank replied.

"It is eating Meester Robers plants," Tito said as his

black eyes squinted accusingly. "I believe it ees from jore yard."

Frank looked toward the bay window facing the back yard. "Why? Is he carrying some sort of identification with this address on it?" Frank smiled. "There are ways of dealing with snails you know. You can sprinkle salt on them or set up beer traps…"

"Meester Beal!" Tito glared at him. "Please, stop sending jore snails to Meester Robers yard or else…things… may… happen."

Frank rose to his full height, and he puffed out his chest. "Yeah? What things?"

Tito dropped the snail at Frank's feet and turned on his heel. "If jew keep sending snails, jew weel find out, but jew don want to know," he warned over his shoulder.

Frank watched him get into his pick up truck and ease away from the curb. He watched until he was down the street and out of sight.

First Robert's new car and now his gardener. At the last neighborhood social, Robert's bragged that he had hired Brazilian gardener, or as he called him a seedsman. One who could grow a virtual Shangri-La. And except for the substantial destruction caused by a nasty infestation of lawn snails he seemed to be doing a pretty good job.

Frank strolled back to his piano and sat down, closed his eyes and took some deep breaths. What would make someone knock ten people down to get to get to a tin of shoe polish? He thought of the basic elements that make people buy products. Saving time, saving money, health, protection or keeping up with the Jones's. He chuckled. In his case, it was keeping up with the Joans's. Between his wife, Joan, and Robert's wife, Joan, maintaining one-upmanship was a full time job.

He tinkled the keys and sighed. Nothing. It wasn't easy to paint a picture with a tune. A tune with meaningful words no less. Be funny, but not too funny, be clever but not for the sake of being clever, and never be a clown. People don't buy things from clowns. He massaged his fingers into his forehead. No Use.

Frank stood and walked to the closet. He opened the door and picked up his tennis racquet from the floor. Time to relax, he thought. This would get his juices flowing. He walked to the sliding glass door and stepped into the backyard. The grass was in need of a mow, and the flowerbeds had lost some of their definition but it was still the biggest yard on the block. He took a couple of practice swings and walked across the flagstone patio to stand next to the barbeque grill. He pulled the cool morning air into his lungs and watched a couple of sparrows quarreling over a slimy bug.

Frank stepped over to a large aquarium and tapped on the side of the glass. "Hello my voracious herbivores." He sprinkled in some fish pellets and watched his belly-footed pets sluggishly feeling their way around. The sides of the aquarium fogged as the morning sun warmed their mossy bed.

He slid a large Ramshorn snail from the side of the glass and held it up. "You are ripe for duty." He raised his tennis racket and held up the snail. "Now go get the breakfast of champions," he said as his racquet met the shell with a pong sound. The snail sailed neatly over the cinder block fence into Roberts' back yard. He removed several more snails from the aquarium and served them over the fence as well.

# Chapter Two

"It has a 289 V8 engine, more than enough power to take you and that beautiful family of yours anywhere you want to go," the car salesman beamed.

"We'll take it," Joan said as she inspected the wood veneer along the side of the station wagon.

"Honey," Frank laughed uncomfortably. "We need some time to talk about this, it's a major purchase," he said to the salesman.

The salesman gave him an acquiescent nod.

Matt bounced enthusiastically behind the steering wheel making engine noises with his mouth. Frank took Joan by the elbow and guided her to the other side of the car. "Let's discuss this."

Joan frowned. "What's to discuss? It's a Ranch Custom wagon."

"So?" Frank frowned.

She smiled deliciously and squeezed her arms around his middle and pressed up against him. Emerald eyes met his hazel. "So," she said as she kissed underneath his jaw. "Joan and Rex Roberts will be green with envy."

Frank frowned. He was beginning to wonder if it wouldn't be easier to murder the Roberts' instead of spending money they didn't have to make them jealous.

"That's a lot of green to slap down to create more of the color green," he replied.

"Don't you just love the smell of a new car though?" Joan asked with a hopeful expression.

"Within two weeks it's going to smell like the old one, an odorous combination of French fries, pizza and Matt's science projects," Frank argued.

Joan sighed. "You only go around once in life, you've got to grab all the gusto you can."

Frank scratched his head. "But why does gusto have to be so expensive?"

Joan looked at the salesman. "We'll take it," she said again.

"Great!" The salesman clapped his hands together. "Let's get the paperwork started." He motioned for them to follow him to the sales office.

"Where's Susan?" Joan's eyes scanned the showroom.

Frank ran tired fingers over his dark short-cropped hair. "My guess is she's underneath the car checking the brakes."

"Folks!" The salesman raised an arm and called from the sales office.

Frank pulled Matt from behind the steering wheel before they marched into the sales office.

"Have you seen our daughter?" Joan asked as she stepped into the office and sat down.

"I'm here, Mother," Susan said from behind. She walked up to the salesman and coolly tore the top sheet from her clipboard. "I've found a fire hazard in your coffee room." Her yellow hard hat seemed to take on an even more official gleam.

He hesitatingly took the paper and looked at her with surprise.

"Do you know it isn't safe to repair a frayed cord with black sticky tape?" She shook her head. "Either replace the cord, or buy a new percolator within two weeks, or I will have to report you to the fire department."

The salesman looked at Frank and Joan. They smiled and shrugged in unison.

\* \* \*

"We'll have to bring Susan every time we buy a new car," Joan said as she ran her hand over the smooth vinyl seats.

Frank nodded. "I have to admit he came down quite a bit on the price."

"I'm hungry," Matt whined from the back.

Joan looked over at Frank. "I didn't plan dinner."

Frank turned his head to look at Matt. "What do you feel like eating?"

"Hamburgers!"

Susan groaned. "How can you eat something that you can't watch them make? I mean, how do you know the people who work in those hamburger joints don't put something disgusting in it?"

"Susan, please," Joan said with a wince. "Fine, we'll go to a restaurant. We'll go to the Red Barn."

"How do you know what they put in *their* hamburgers?"

"Susan, it's a nice steak house, they aren't going to put disgusting things in your food."

"But how do you know?"

"I know," Frank lied. "I asked them once and it seems it's an all beef patty, special sauce, lettuce, cheese, pickles and onions on a sesame seed bun."

Susan was quiet for a moment. "What's in the special sauce?"

"What do you think is in it?" Joan turned to glare at Susan in the back seat.

Susan shrugged. "That's the point. I don't know what's inside the bun."

"Maybe you should learn to think outside the bun," Joan suggested.

"Man, this power steering is great," Frank said as he turned into the parking lot of the Red Barn.

"I want to drive home," Joan said. "After all, buying a new car was my idea."

Frank eased into a parking space. "Have it your way."

They walked backwards toward the door to admire their shiny new car. The light was dim inside the restaurant compared to the bright lights of the parking lot. Frank nodded to the piano player out of professional courtesy as they walked to their booth. The sawdust on the floor instantly reminded him of the places he and his brother used to frequent as teenagers back in Indiana.

The moment they were seated Joan dug a dollar from her purse. "Matt, give this to the piano player and ask him to play my favorite song."

"Aw mom, I don't even know how to say it," Matt whined.

Susan pushed her face close to his. "It's Lisbon

Antigua."

Matt shoved her back. "Keep your cooties away from me."

"Susan, since you know how to say it," Joan said and handed her the dollar, "you do the honors."

Susan let out a huge sigh and rolled her eyes. "Fine." She slid out of the booth.

"Susan," Frank said.

She turned to give him a wry look. "What?"

"Why don't you leave the hard hat here?"

Susan took off her hat and sat it on the booth before shuffling off, kicking at the sawdust as she walked.

"You don't have to pay to hear that song you know," Frank said to Joan. "I'll play it for you anytime you want."

Joan smiled dryly. "You say it, but you don't do it." She lifted the menu to cover her face. "All you do is play those silly jingles of yours."

A flush heated Franks face. "I see." He cleared the anger from his throat. "Those silly jingles Joan?"

She lowered her menu.

"They are paying for this meal, our new car, the clothes we're wearing and the roof over our heads."

Matt looked up at the ceiling.

"Of course dear," Joan said and gave his arm a condescending pat. "And my little worthless part-time job pays for nothing."

The tinkling keys of the piano began to play Lisbon Antigua.

"Did I say that?" Frank growled.

The waiter appeared next to the table. "May I get

you some beverages while you make your selection?"

"Yeah, I'd like a double martini," Frank announced.

"Frank," Joan said in a warning tone. "You're driving."

"No dear, you are." He looked back at the waiter. "Make that a triple martini."

"Dad, can I have a Roy Rogers?" Matt asked.

Frank nodded. "A Roy Rogers for my son and two cokes.

"I'll just have a cup of coffee please," Joan said.

The waiter quickly wrote down their requests and walked away.

"Since when do you drink coffee at night?" Frank glared at Joan.

"I've just started. Besides, coffee is cheaper than coke."

Frank ground his teeth. "For God's sake Joan, I can afford to buy you a coke!"

"I don't want one." She raised her menu back up.

"I want to buy you a coke," Frank raised his voice, and several people looked over at them.

Joan slapped her menu down on the table. "You can buy the whole world a coke and keep it company for all I care!" She pushed Frank to stand then slid out of the booth and stomped toward the ladies room.

Frank gulped in deep breaths as he listened to the piano player end the song with a flourish.

"Dad, how much does the roof over our heads cost?" Matt looked up again.

The waiter returned with their drinks followed closely by a chef with his arm around Susan's shoulders.

"Sir," the chef began. "Is this your daughter?"

Frank took a swig of his martini before answering. "Yes sir, she is."

"Please inform her that this is the area for guests, and the kitchen is reserved for the cooks."

"Daddy, you should see how dirty the kitchen is, there's food lying everywhere, and the aprons they're wearing are disgusting," she said as she pointed to the cook's front. Her face twisted up. "And I think I saw a dead bug on the floor."

"Shhh!" The chef held a finger to his lips. "That's my pet bug," he whispered. "His name is Herman. Now I'll have to go revive him. We bring good things to life you know. Please don't scare him again." He shook his head and walked away.

"Susan, sit!" Frank commanded. He looked up at the waiter. "We'll have two New York steaks, medium rare with baked potatoes, butter and sour cream and two dinner salads." He looked over at Matt and Susan. "They will both have a hamburger with fries."

"Very good, sir."

Susan watched the waiter walk toward the kitchen then sipped at her coke. She gave Frank a snotty look. "You think it's butter but it's not."

"Susan, that's enough," Frank said before taking another gulp of his martini.

Joan returned and sat down in the booth without saying a word.

"I ordered you a steak with a baked potato and salad," Frank said with a friendly tone. "Is that alright?"

"Why are you asking me? You know what you can

afford and what you can't," Joan snapped.

Frank knew better than to try to keep the conversation going when Joan was in one of her moods. Her monthly cycle maybe? Whether it was or whether it wasn't, he was smart enough to keep quiet.

"You want me to ask the piano player to play something else?" Matt asked as pushed his fingers into his glass and fished out two maraschino cherries.

Frank gulped more of his drink and pushed a hand in his pocket. "Yeah, ask him to play *Always*. Can you say that?" He grinned.

"Hah! Very funny, dad." Matt dried his sticky hand on his white crisp napkin and plucked the dollar from Frank's fingers. He disappeared beneath the table.

"Matthew Beal! That's no way to leave the table," Joan chided. But he was already on his way toward the piano player.

Frank drained the rest of his martini. He held the glass up to signal the waiter. The waiter nodded and returned to the table.

"Another triple martini please."

"Right away, sir." He picked up Frank's glass from the table. Frank grabbed his arm as he turned.

"Don't take my olive," he slurred slightly as he pinched the toothpick from the edge of the glass and popped the olive into his mouth.

"Yes sir," the waiter said.

Joan leaned toward Frank after the waiter walked away. "Don't you think you've had enough?"

Frank sat quietly for a moment, eyes closed, swaying as he listened to the arrangement of *Always* floating from the piano player's direction. "They played this song at our wedding," he reminisced and placed a hand over Joan's before heaving a sigh. "I'm glad we were able to book that band before the lead singer was electrocuted by the faulty wiring on his amplifier." He cracked an eye and flicked her a sidelong glance to catch a faint smile on her face.

Joan was usually impressed when he remembered a heartwarming detail. He felt her staring at the side of his face.

"They played it at our reception," she corrected then pulled her hand back and sipped her coffee. "And it wasn't the singer who was electrocuted, it was the guitarist."

Frank's eyes snapped open as if an alarm clock had just gone off. He took a pen from his shirt pocket and began to scribble something on his cocktail napkin.

"What are you writing?" Susan tried to cock her head so she could see.

Frank grinned. "I have an idea for the ad I'm working on."

# Chapter Three

"Dad, are we getting a dog?"

Frank cracked an eye to see Matt dressed and ready for school.

"Hmm?" Frank licked an arid tongue over his chapped lips. "A dog? Where would you get an idea like that?" He mumbled and squeezed his eyes shut to keep out the evil morning sunlight lurking just on the other side of his hangover.

"Last night you asked the waiter to give you a doggie bag so I thought we were getting a dog."

"No Matt, no dog," Frank groaned and rolled his face into his pillow.

"But why?" Matt asked with a longing that would require more than any parent's *because I said so* response.

Frank slowly unwound himself from his pillow and the bedding and shoved his legs over the side of the bed. With a hand on each knee, he hung his head. It was as if a sledgehammer had smashed on a pedestal at his feet, sending a marker ripping through every nerve ending in his spinal column. A sharp bell rang in his head and ricochet painfully off the walls of his skull. Bingo! He had won first prize. The gigantic, plush, stuffed toy.

He reached forward and tugged Matt down to sit on the edge of the mattress. "Son, do you remember what happened to Hamlet?"

A look of protest washed over Matt's face. "Dad, that was months ago."

Frank winced at the volume of Matt's voice. "Nevertheless, you didn't take care of him, and he went legs up," he said as softly as he could.

The door of the bedroom opened. "There you are," Joan said. "We have to go or you'll be late for school."

"Mom," Matt whined. "Tell dad a dog is different than a hamster."

A slow smile spread across Joan's face. "If I have to tell your father that, he had way more to drink last night than I thought."

Frank squinted up at her. "Sorry about that." He scrubbed his hands hard over his face. "I guess I got carried away celebrating our new car."

"No kidding, you almost got carried away by two of the waiters after you insisted on filling in for the piano player during his break time."

Frank vaguely remembered singing a rousing rendition of 'when the saints come marching in' among other party tunes.

Matt grinned. "I thought you were neato, dad."

"Come on Matt," Joan said and turned. She stopped suddenly and returned. She rummaged through the contents of her purse and pulled out a cocktail napkin. "I almost forgot." She handed it to Frank. "Here are your ideas for the ad you're working on."

Frank swallowed a gag and took it from her fingers. He blinked and tried to focus on the tattered napkin, he turned it over then back again. He stared at it with cotton-headed shock. It was filled with the illegible scrawling of a frustrated jingle writer.

"By the way," Joan said. "We're having Melinda's boyfriend for dinner tonight. I thought we may as well get to know him so we'll know what we're up against." She bent down and softly kissed his cheek.

Frank nodded dumbly and held his breath for fear that Joan's heavily applied Madame Rochas perfume would send him racing to the bathroom.

The house was finally empty; everyone had gone to their designated regions. It was his favorite time of day, the most productive time of day, morning. Frank stood in front of the bathroom mirror, it reported back accurately the way he felt. He opened the medicine chest and browsed the contents.

"Ah yes," he said as he reached for the Alka Seltzer. "My friend Speedy." He gazed at the character on the box before opening it. It smiled back at him, wearing an effervescent tablet as a hat. He removed one of the foil packets. "Now why couldn't I have thought of that?" He tore open the packet and let the large tablets plunk into his palm. "Plop, plop, fizz, fizz," he said as he held one of the tablets over his head halo style. He gave his reflection a disappointed glare. He looked around for the rinsing glass. It was gone.

"I swear," he said as he headed down the stairs. "Why don't things stay where they belong?" He walked into the kitchen and opened a cupboard. It was empty. The sink was full of dishes. "Three kids and a wife and not one of them do any dishes." He turned around and leaned his backside against the edge of the counter then looked up at the ceiling in desperation. He shrugged, and as he popped both Alka Seltzer tablets into his mouth, the doorbell rang.

The fizzing didn't get a good rolling start until after he had his hand on the knob. He opened the door and wasn't altogether surprised to see Tito Tortuga standing on his porch.

"Meester Beal," Tito began. "I tole jew jesterday to stop sending jore snails into Meester Robers jard."

Frank quickly tried to swallow the foam as it churned. At first he was successful but the volume soon ballooned and tripled, the tablets began producing much more than he could swallow. The effervescent white muck began to seep out of the corner of his mouth and run down his chin.

Tito frowned. "Are jew rabid?"

"Wha?" Frank asked with his head tipped back so he wouldn't drip on the floor.

"Are jew sick?" He repeated.

Frank swallowed and coughed. He wiped at the steadily flowing froth curving from the corners of his mouth. He shook his head and began to close the door. Tito blocked it with the toe of his shoe.

"I tole jew Meester Beal." He shook his head sadly. "I tole jew a hundred tines, but jew don lisson." He reached in and grabbed Frank's wrist and pulled his arm out. "Now jew weel fine out what things may happen." He put a snail into Frank's hand, closed it then wrapped both of his hands tightly around it. He squeezed until Frank felt the snail's shell shatter and the slick texture of its moist body.

"Gawwk!" Frank yelled and ground his teeth breaking the tablets into numerous foaming pieces. He jerked his hand back and shook away the mess. "Go away!" Frank managed to yell and slammed the door before running into the downstairs bathroom and spitting what was left of the tablets into the sink. He stood red-faced and panting as he scrubbed the snail from his hand and rinsed out his mouth.

"This means war!" He vowed into the mirror. He stomped back to the kitchen and picked up the phone. He dialed a number and listened.

"Gene, I need your help," he said staring at his palm as if the snail were still there. "Yes. Yes. Okay, we'll leave the light on for you." He hung up and stomped out onto the back patio.

Frank mimicked Arthur Ashe's style as best he could. He twirled his racquet and served several snails, ripe or not, into Robert's back yard before he was able to calm down.

A number of aspirin later, Frank settled down to work. Same old quandary, same old block. Maybe he had picked up a virus? Matt was always bringing something home from school. Macaroni cuff links, paper mache Christmas ornaments, relief maps of the United States made from flour, salt and water and on special days, bronchial pneumonia.

He played two rounds of chopsticks then blew out a breath. His thoughts wandered back to Roberts and his strange Brazilian gardener. Imagine Roberts thinking his yard could be the cream of the crop? First one on the block to have a blue ribbon, first prize, showcase backyard. He snorted. Everyone knows it's what's up front that counts.

Perhaps he should have checked with Joan before inviting Gene? He shook his head. If she got angry, and put up a fuss, he knew exactly what he would tell her.

\* \* \*

"I'm sorry," Frank said. "I just wasn't thinking."

"That's an understatement, I'd say," Joan glared. "Don't you remember all the trouble we had the last time he came to visit?"

"He's my brother." Frank shrugged. "I was angry."

"What exactly did this Brazilian gardener say to you to get you so angry?"

Susan walked in, her steps slowed when she felt the energy of the mood in the kitchen.

He said things...may...happen, Frank impersonated a Brazilian accent. "Then he crushed a snail in my hand."

"That's assault," Susan chimed in. "Assault with a deadly weapon, punishable by law."

"Susan please," Joan said. "A snail is hardly a deadly weapon."

Susan turned to Frank. "Was it a poisonous snail?"

"Susan, this is a private conversation between your father and me."

Susan gave Joan a bored glance and opened the cupboard to get a glass.

Joan moved away from the sink so Susan could get a full view of the pile of dirty dishes. "If you insist on staying in the room, I'm going to make you wash the dishes."

Susan looked at the dishes, then back at Joan. "Let

me know when dinner is ready." She quickly made an about face and walked out.

Joan focused her stare back on Frank. "What is Gene doing now?"

Frank shrugged. "He's looking for work. He just hasn't found the right job."

"In all of my imagination," Joan opened her arms wide. "I can't think of any profession that would be right for Gene. Why is he out of work this time?"

"Deadwood," Frank replied.

"Is that where he lives now?" Joan's voice raised an octave.

"No, it's what he became. They bought machines to do what Gene was doing."

Joan turned on the water in the sink and began yanking the dishes out of the sink one by one.

"And just what was Gene doing when all the machines took over?" She dropped a glass. It shattered and shards went in all directions across the floor. She looked at Frank as if he had knocked it from her hand before bending down to pick up the pieces.

Frank went to the utility room to get the whiskbroom and dustpan.

"Move," he said and began sweeping up the glass.

Matt came bouncing into the kitchen, full of energy and smiles. "What's for dinner?" he asked before stepping on a sliver of glass.

"Aaagh," he yelled hopping on one foot.

"Matt, get out of here, there's broken glass on the floor," Joan ordered, holding up a hand.

Matt hobbled to one of the kitchen chairs. "I got

some in my foot!" he wailed.

"I'll go get the tweezers," Joan said and rushed out of the kitchen.

Frank walked over to Matt. "How did you get glass in your foot? You're wearing your tennis shoes."

Matt grinned up at Frank. "You looked like you needed me to rescue you."

Frank gave him a fatherly look. "Matt, it's not your job to rescue me, and besides, what makes you think I needed to be rescued from your mom?"

"You had that *help me* look," Matt said with a shrug. "I thought if I helped you then you would help me."

"What is a *help me* look?" Frank asked.

Matt displayed a helpless expression.

Frank frowned. "You want me to rescue you from mom?"

Matt waved a hand. "I don't need rescuing from mom. I know how to handle her." He reached down to take off his shoe and sock.

"Then what do you need help with?" Frank asked curiously.

"I need help gettin' a dog."

Frank's face seized with a dumfounded look.

Joan appeared carrying a first aid kit and a needle. "Which foot is it?" She kneeled down.

"Thanks mom," he said pulling his sock back on. "Dad already got it out." Matt looked up at Frank and raised his eyebrows up and down.

# Chapter Four

"How do I look?" Melinda asked, and then twirled around.

Joan sized her up. "Except for the dangling caterpillars under your eyes and the blue satin blouse, you could pass for a vagrant."

Melinda turned away. "What are we having for dinner?"

"Roast beef, mashed potatoes with gravy, brown and serve rolls and corn, the same thing we always have on Tuesday night," Joan replied. "And please tell me you're not going to wear those holey jeans."

"Mother!" Melinda squeaked. "What's Bobby going to eat? I told you he's a vegetarian."

"You did no such thing," Joan shot back. "He's too young to be a vegetarian anyway."

"Can't you at least make a salad?" Melinda whined.

Joan put her hands on her hips. "I could, but unless you do it, Bobby's going to eat corn and rolls for dinner."

"Fine!" Melinda pulled a head of lettuce and three tomatoes from the refrigerator. She took a large bowl from the cupboard and began tearing lettuce leaves into it. She cut the tomatoes in quarters with exaggerated chopping sounds and sprinkled them on top of the mound of lettuce.

Joan peeked over Melinda's shoulder. "Why are you using the popcorn bowl for salad? Why don't you use the salad bowl?"

"Is it going to taste different if I use this bowl for the salad?" Melinda asked with a snooty tone.

"You know very well we use the big brown plastic bowl for popcorn and the clear glass bowl for salad," Joan insisted.

Melinda jerked around. "Why?" She stepped over to the refrigerator and took out some green onions, a cucumber and an avocado.

"Because I don't want my plastic bowl to smell like onions, that's why," Joan raised her voice. "Do you like onion flavored popcorn?"

"Then I won't use onions," Melinda said and put the onions back on the shelf.

"Just use the glass bowl!" Joan ordered.

"Mother, this is my salad!"

"Melinda, this is my kitchen!"

Melinda burst into tears. "Why does everyone in this family get their way except for me?" She ran out of the kitchen and stomped up the stairs.

Joan shook her head and jerked the glass bowl from the cupboard. She dumped the half made salad into it and rinsed out the plastic bowl and dried it before putting it away.

"Do we have hormones on the warpath?" Frank asked from behind.

"I wish you'd talk to her," Joan pleaded. "We seem to be speaking two different languages these days."

"What do you want me to say?" Frank asked.

"You'd better say *something* before she cries those caterpillars right off her face."

Frank slipped an arm around Joan's shoulder and gave her a compassionate look. "Honey, is it really that important to have the salad in this particular bowl?" He glanced at the glass bowl.

"Oh I see, this is all *my* fault," Joan returned.

Frank's eyebrows knitted. "That's not what I'm saying. It's just that at this very impressionable time in her life it might be good to allow her to make some choices for herself."

"Impressionable?" Joan stepped back to gaze at him. "What about me? What about how all of this is impressing me?" Her lower lip began to tremble. A tear welled up and rolled down her cheek to drip onto the bib of her apron. "I go to work every day, I cook, I clean, I wash clothes, and I take the kids where they want to go. What thanks do I get? I may as well wear a horse harness everyday."

"No!" Frank lowered arms around her waist and pulled her close. "Don't talk like that.

"But you're accusing me of being an ogre, someone who abuses her children. What must the neighbors think? Does she or doesn't she?" She wept.

"They don't think any such thing, we have wonderful kids." Frank gently tipped her head back and thumbed the tears from her cheeks. "The neighbors are probably wondering what we think." He kissed her nose then softly kissed her lips.

The doorbell rang.

"That must be Bobby," Frank said.

Joan stepped back and took a deep breath. "I'll be fine." She cleared her throat and pulled a paper towel from the roll.

Frank turned on the porch light and tentatively peeked out the curtain before opening the door.

The young man was wearing a white tee shirt. The fringed brown vest partially covered the big yellow smiley face on the front of his shirt. His threadbare blue jeans wouldn't have upset Frank except that he was wearing his hair long as well, all the way past his ear lobes.

"Bobby," Frank said as he extended his hand. "You can leave your skate board outside."

Bobby looked at Frank's hand as if he didn't know what to do with it, and then finally gave it a shake "Mr. Beal?"

"Melinda will be down in a minute."

Bobby sniffed at the air and curled his upper lip. "Meat?"

"Roast beef night," Frank said proudly.

Bobby wandered around the living room picking up knick-knacks and nodding knowingly. "I haven't eaten anything with a face since I was six," he said.

"Me either," Frank said. "I'm more of a rump man myself."

Bobby gave him a half smile and flopped down on the couch. He smoothed a hand over the splashy design on mustard color velveteen fabric. "Nice couch, my parents have one just like it in green."

Frank turned and stared at him through narrowed eyes. "Have a seat." He walked over and sat down in his recliner directly across from Bobby. He smiled, leaned back and laced his fingers behind his head. "What else do they have?"

Bobby gazed around the room. "Pretty much the same stuff." His eyes stopped at the piano. "Except for the piano. They don't have one of those." He looked back at Frank. "And my dad doesn't wear a jacket in the house." Bobby's gaze dropped down to Frank's Nehru jacket.

"Groovy," Frank said and smiled.

Bobby frowned slightly then smiled uncomfortably.

"Hello," Melinda said cheerfully as she clomped down the stairs.

Bobby's head jerked up in her direction. "Hey Mel."

"Is Daddy giving you the third degree?" she asked as she plopped down beside Bobby and threw a leg over his.

Frank leaned forward and wasted no time bringing his recliner into an upright position. "Melinda?" He waited until he had Melinda's full attention. "Would you like to put a respectable distance between you and Bobby before your mother comes in?"

"Oh, Daddy, you're so old fashioned." She giggled.

An edgy, concerned tension seemed to suck all the air out of the room. Up until the present moment, Frank saw Melinda through fatherly eyes, like he always had. Daddy's little girl. All of a sudden he became aware that she wasn't a little girl anymore, far from it. What bothered him more was the most obvious; Bobby didn't see her as a little girl either.

"Dinner's ready," Joan said as she stepped into the

living room. Frank turned to see her reaction to Melinda and Bobby pretzled up together on the couch. He watched her blink at them with the slightest confusion. "Melinda, would you like to help me get dinner on the table?"

"Sure mom." Melinda untangled herself and hopped up from the couch. All the previous signs of hormone turmoil had disappeared. It seemed Bobby possessed the neutralizing agent for severe mood swings in the form of his own brand of hormone therapy.

"I'll round up Susan and Matt," Frank said as he headed for the front door.

* * *

Moods lightened as they all gathered around the dinner table and proceeded to their usual places.

"You take this seat Bobby," Joan said as she pushed an empty chair next to her.

Frank looked at Melinda as she groaned audibly. He gave her a questioning frown.

"The interrogation chair," she whispered to him.

Frank's head leaned back as an understanding expression sequestered his face.

"Bobby, what are your plans after high school?" Joan asked as she smoothed her napkin across her lap.

"I'm going to enter some skateboarding contests unless I get drafted," he said as his eyes perused the banquet in front of him.

Joan offered him the platter of sliced beef.

Bobby held up a hand. "No thanks. I don't eat meat." He reached for the bowl of sliced carrots. "I love vegetables though. They're magically delicious."

"What's magic about a vegetable?" Matt asked.

"Think about it," Bobby replied as he scooped large spoonfuls onto his plate. "They have all the vitamins and nutrients you need, and they grow right out of the dirt."

Susan stared at him. "The American Medical association says skateboarding accidents are the leading cause of head injuries."

Bobby smiled. "That's because amateurs don't know how to ride them."

"Are you planning on college at all?" Joan asked.

"Society places too much emphasis on education," Bobby said as he piled a heap of salad on his plate.

"Society?" Frank looked puzzled. "What land do you live in?"

An arrogant smile spread across Bobby's face. "Yes, there's way too much emphasis on conformity, and America has become much too materialistic and competitive."

Frank reared back in mock horror. "Easy to say while you're roughing it in your parents' house in the suburbs."

"It's a new world, Daddy," Melinda added. "It's time to tune in, turn on and drop out."

"Turn on?" Joan asked. "You're not experimenting with drugs are you?" Her face fell with concern.

"Oh, Mother, it's a figure of speech," Melinda replied with distain.

"Besides, there are many more ways of building self esteem than surviving a four year college," Bobby added.

"Self esteem is no substitute for a good education young man," Frank snapped.

Susan contemplated her scoop of mashed potatoes. "It's because the wheels are made of clay isn't it?"

"What wheels?" Matt asked.

"On skateboards dummy," Susan said with a sneer.

"None of that kind of talk young lady," Joan scolded.

Susan looked at Bobby. "The clay wheels don't grip very well, and it causes accidents doesn't it?"

Bobby shrugged. "Got milk?" he asked Joan.

"I thought you were a vegetarian," Frank said.

"I am," Bobby said with a nod.

"So, you won't eat the cow but you'll drink what's inside it?" Frank stabbed his fork in the air.

"As long as I don't have to milk it," Bobby added.

Frank looked at Bobby in the eye. "I see. It's kind of like spending the materialistic, competitive fruits of your parent's labor but refusing to go out and make it yourself."

"No way Mr. Beal," Bobby shook his head. "I'm gonna make lots of money in the skateboard competitions." He scooped up a spoonful of mashed potatoes and tapped them onto his plate. "Sure, I've broken an arm and a couple of fingers but all in all, I think it's going to pay off in the end." He set the bowl down and licked his thumb. "Just do it!" He dipped his head and shoveled potatoes into his mouth. "That's what I always say." He could barely get the words out of his full mouth.

"Just how much money can you make riding a board with wheels?" Joan smirked.

Bobby nearly choked on his salad. "Two words Mrs. Beal." He smiled at Melinda. "Hobie Alter." He nodded his head as though the secrets of the Universe had just been revealed to them.

"What kind of Alter?" Joan gave him a puzzled look.

"He's talking about that surf bum," Frank said.

Bobby scowled at Frank. "Bum?" He chuckled. "Try millionaire bum. He not only made millions by making surf boards and catamarans, now he's teamed up with Vita-Pakt juice company to sell his skateboards."

Frank eyed him with a superior expression. "I thought you were against a competitive, materialistic warped society."

Bobby exchanged a knowing glance with Melinda and smiled. "Just like Doctor Eric Berne says." He buttered a roll and pushed half of it into his mouth.

"What? Doctor who?" Frank looked around the table for an answer.

"Doctor Berne, Daddy," Melinda said matter of factly. "He wrote 'Games People Play."

"So?" The look on Frank's face was priceless. "What games are we playing? Parcheesi? Tiddlywinks? Monopoly?"

Matt spit his milk out on his plate and laughed a genuine, big toothed, head thrown back belly laugh. He sputtered and sprayed milk into the air as he held on to his stomach.

"Oh, my God!" Susan hitched her chair away from Matt's until she sat at the opposite corner of the table. "You are such a ditz!"

Joan frowned and half rose from her chair. "Matt, for heaven's sake." She looked at Susan. "No name calling young lady."

"Okay mom, don't have a cow," Susan replied.

A snort sounded behind them, and they all turned their heads.

"Gene!" Frank yelled.

Matt's face lit up, and he jumped up from his chair to greet him then he suddenly stopped in his tracks.

"Dad? Why is Uncle Gene wearing a skirt?"

# Chapter Five

"My number is two; my Tartan is blue, and a royal descendant from the clan of Blackethouse." Uncle Gene gave them a toothless grin. "It's a kilt son, not a skirt."

"Hey Brother Gene," Frank said smiling, and he stood to greet him with a hug and three solid pats on the back.

Gene was a slight man, a smidge shorter than Frank. He had lost his teeth after contracting a serious gum disease while in the Navy and despite the encouragement of family and dental professionals, he staunchly refused to wear his dentures. His gums were tough enough though and with the repeated application of one- hundred proof scotch, they performed as well as any teeth in the tearing and grinding of food.

"Hello Gene," Joan said coolly. She gave his attire an evaluating look.

"Well, if it isn't the fair Joan, light of my brother's life." He walked over to give her a stiff hug.

"Would you like to join us for dinner?" she asked.

Gene gazed around the table. "It appears that I have come to where the flavor is."

"I'll get you a chair," Frank said and walked to the next room.

"How long has it been?" Gene asked as he looked at

each of the children. "Melinda, is that you?"

Melinda gave him an embarrassed smile and exchanged a glance with Bobby. "And Susan!" Gene's eyes widened. "I'd hardly recognize you. How old are you now? Ten?"

Susan tilted her head back proudly. "I'm twelve."

"Are you now?" His hazel eyes glittered with mirth since it had only been six months since he had come to visit.

"Is that official Scottish clothes you're wearing?" Susan asked.

Gene walked around the table and stood next to Matt. "You must be Matt. Why I remember when you were born, you were only a wee bit longer than a newborn pup." He ruffled the top of Matt's hair.

"Here Gene, sit here. Matt, move your chair over." Frank sat the chair down.

Joan handed him a dinner plate and utensils, and Gene sat between Matt and Frank.

Gene sniffed. "It's been a long time since I've had a sit down dinner with family."

"Where's Helen?" Frank asked curiously.

Gene shrugged as he placed several slices of roast beef on his plate. "She's gone now," he whispered and shook his head sadly.

"Good God Gene, we didn't know." Frank slipped an arm around his brother's shoulders. "Why didn't you call? We would have come to see you."

"I don't like to burden anyone with my problems."

"That's what family is for," Frank insisted. "When we were kids we stuck up for each other. We seemed to sense when the other was in some kind of trouble, and we were right there for each other. Remember when I was in sixth grade, and you were in fifth?" Frank looked around the table to make sure everyone was listening. "One day after school, the Thompson brother's and a bunch of their friends decided they were going to beat us up. They chased us for five blocks before one of them hooked his finger in my belt loop and threw me on the ground." Frank gave Gene a proud look. "Gene jumped them with fists flying and a war yell that could have woke the dead." Frank said somberly. "They still beat us up but I remember how proud I was to be Gene's brother. There wasn't anything we wouldn't do for each other back then." Frank frowned. "What's changed?"

Joan's face held a guilty expression. "How did she go Gene?" she asked softly.

Gene slathered several spoons of gravy over his meat and mashed potatoes.

"Greyhound I think, or maybe it was the El Capitan. She loved to travel by train. She ran off with a lingerie salesman who was passing through town. She warned me if I didn't start wearing my teeth and slow down on the drinking she would leave." He shrugged as he poured dressing on his salad. "Guess she wasn't kidding." He scooped up a fork full of mashed potatoes and held it up in front of him. "Through the gums, look out stomach, here it comes." The potatoes disappeared into the dark cavern beneath his nose, and Gene rolled his eyes to the ceiling as he chewed. "M'm, M'm good!"

Joan glared at Gene then shifted her gaze to Frank.

"Uncle Gene," Susan said. "You didn't answer my

question."

"What question was that darlin'?" he asked as he sopped a puddle of gravy with a piece of roll.

"Is that official Scottish clothes you're wearing?"

"If you mean authentic, yes it is," he said between bites. "In the old country, they used Tartans...or the weave of a man's plaid as a means of identification."

"The old country? You mean Indiana?" Matt asked innocently. "Dad says you're from Indiana."

"Older than that," Gene said with a laugh that exposed his last bite of carrots. "The lineage of this family goes back to the thirteenth century, Scotland." He wiped his mouth with the heal of his hand. "Our name is derived from the French 'Bel' meaning fair or handsome." He smiled at Matt. "Aye, we were a turbulent mix of French and Scottish families throughout the fifteenth and sixteenth centuries."

"Honest? We had wars and stuff?"

"Aye son."

"Didn't you say there was royalty in our family tree?" Susan asked excitedly.

Gene dipped his head and shifted his eyes from Susan to Frank with glee. "General Sir John Bell was a distinguished soldier, and a friend of the Duke of Ellington."

Gene and Frank burst into laughter in unison.

Suddenly Gene stopped laughing and blinked across the table at Bobby. "Who is this lad?"

"This is Melinda's friend, Bobby MacCormack," Frank announced. "A new addition to the neighborhood."

Gene jerked to his feet causing his chair to topple over. "MacCormack?! A long time enemy of the clan of Beal's." He shoved an index finger into the air. "Much pain and loss was caused by the MacCormack clan forcing the Beal ancestors to move many miles to the north of Scotland, a place where beauty and ugly wouldn't have to stand in opposition. He bared his gums. "Where has your ugly clan settled now?" His eyes burned into Bobby's.

"I'm from across the street," Bobby stuttered.

Frank stooped down and picked up Gene's chair. He sat it back on its legs behind Gene. "Calm down brother." He patted Gene on the shoulder. "Bobby doesn't have any recollection of the events of five centuries ago."

"There's a piece of them in every cell of his body," Gene said nodding accusingly. He slowly sat back down never taking his eyes from Bobby's. "What does your ugly father do for a living?"

"He's a schoolteacher," Bobby replied.

Gene nodded knowingly. "That figures, the MacCormack's were always finding ways of spreading their foul propaganda among the youth."

"My father teaches biology Mr. Beal." Bobby gave him a tight smile. "I don't think he teaches any foul propaganda."

Gene picked up his butter knife and split another roll. "Tell me Bobby, has he ever dissected a chicken?"

Bobby grinned. "No, my mother usually does that in the kitchen."

"You won't eat it though," Melinda giggled. "Really Uncle Gene, do you have to be so heavy?"

Gene gave her a puzzled look. "I weigh the same now as I did in high school I'll have you know."

Melinda giggled again. "I didn't mean fat, I meant controversial."

"Don't know about that," Gene said as he looked around the table. "So, my fair Joan, what do we have in the way of dessert?"

Joan stared at him. She took a deep breath and expelled it. "I bought a coconut cream pie." She stood and turned to go into the kitchen.

"Well, I'm..." he crossed his eyes..."coo coo for coconut!" Gene hooted.

Matt spit milk on his plate again, and his shoulders shook with coughing and laughter.

Gene slapped Matt on the back several times then crooked a finger under his chin and tipped his head back. "What do you say we take our pie into the living room and watch a bit of television?

"We aren't allowed to eat in the living room," Matt said.

"I'm not surprised with the way you drink your milk," Gene said with a shrug.

Matt howled again and nearly fell off his chair in a fit of laughter.

Susan got up from the table and stood behind Gene. "I'll watch Bewitched with you Uncle Gene."

"Okay lass, go warm up the TV, and I'll be there in a minute."

"I want to watch the Flintstones," Matt said as he followed her into the living room.

"It was nice meeting you," Bobby held out a hand to

Gene.

Gene stared at him for a long moment then took hold of his hand and gave it a beefy squeeze. Bobby winced.

"I'll be watchin you son," Gene warned as he gave Melinda a wink.

Frank waited for everyone to leave the table, and then he eyed Gene. "So, why the sudden interest in the family ancestry?"

Gene shrugged. "I don't know."

Frank frowned. "Are you going to tell me this kilt is now part of your daily attire?"

Gene smiled revealing a large slice of his gums. He chuckled. "No, I only started to wear them last week."

"Why?" Frank asked.

Gene lowered his voice. "I've got a hot rash, and the doctor said I can't wear pants for a couple of weeks." He looked around and leaned closer to Frank. "It's in a delicate spot."

Frank held up a hand. "Go no further; I don't need to know the details."

"It presents an obstacle when looking for work." Gene settled gently back into his chair. "Especially factory work."

"Why did you get fired this time?"

Gene frowned. "What makes you think I got fired?"

Frank flicked him a look.

"Okay, so I took a couple golf clubs. They had thousands. Besides, those damn commies put in a bunch of machines to do all the work we were doing."

"What were you doing with golf clubs?" Frank smirked.

Gene slanted him a glance. "I was puttin' the heads on the shafts for the Big Birdie Driver, at least until they got those fancy machines to do it." He shook his head. "My boss said automation would be able to calculate an accurate forty-five degree angle and seat the head on the shaft in half the time it took workers to get the job done. Double your pleasure, double your fun, that's what he said." Gene muffled a laugh. "I poured a carton of salt in that machine before I left."

Gene gazed at Frank. "So, how can I help you?"

Frank looked puzzled. "Help me?"

"You called me to say you needed some help. What did you need help with?"

# Chapter Six

By the strip of hallway light beneath the bedroom door, Frank stepped out of his pants and hung them over the back of a chair. He snapped his eyes closed when the change from both his front pockets jingled to the floor.

"I'm awake," Joan whispered.

He stepped across the room and slipped under the bed covers. "I'm sorry," he said as he slid next to her drew her close to mold his front to her back. "I didn't mean to wake you."

"What time is it?" she asked.

"Almost one o'clock. Gene and I had a lot of catching up to do."

Joan glanced back at him. "Did he tell you why he is wearing a kilt?"

Frank grinned into the darkness. "He confessed he has a hot rash so he can't wear his pants right now."

Joan's shoulders jiggled with laughter, she pushed her face into her pillow to muffle the sound. She finally came up for air. "All that stuff about the family ancestry," she gasped. "It is an attractive kilt though, I was going to ask him where he got it," she giggled. "They are so slenderizing."

Frank joined her in laughter. "He says it's hard to go on job interviews, especially for factory work."

Joan slapped a hand over her mouth to catch a laugh. She struggled to get the words out. "Maybe he'd have better luck in the secretarial pool."

The bed shook for a long time as they laughed together. Frank smoothed a hand down Joan's arm then leaned over to kiss the side of her neck.

"Frank, I'm worried about Melinda."

Frank lifted himself to one elbow. "She's a teenager; she's supposed to worry you."

"It's hard for me to parent her when we argue all the time," she sighed.

Frank found a lock of Joan's hair and twirled it loosely around his finger. "She's just trying to establish her independence."

"She asked me if she could go to the drive-in with Bobby," Joan suddenly jerked her head around. "Ouch!" Her hair snagged on Frank's finger.

"Sorry," he said and uncoiled the lock. "Would it be so bad to let her go?"

He felt the heat of Joan's glare in the darkness. "Do you know what they want to see?"

Frank shook his head. "I have no idea; I haven't been to the movies in years."

"The Cool Ones!"

He shrugged. "Sounds like it might be fun."

"I don't think Melinda should see a movie about a girl who invents a dance called 'The Tantrum'.

Frank frowned. "How do you know about all this?"

"It's my job to know. I have to stay one step ahead of the kids or else they will use my ignorance against me."

Frank laced his fingers behind his head and settled

back against his pillow. "I had no idea that I was living in the middle of a conspiracy."

"You know what I mean," Joan said.

He rolled toward her and gently massaged her shoulders. "Yes, I do. Don't you remember when we used to go to the drive-in?" He softly kissed her ear. "Popcorn, sodas and those little hard gummy candies you used to love?"

"Is that what you remember?" She put a hand over his. "With all the kissing and heavy breathing," she pulled his hand down. "And the steamed up windows? We couldn't even see the movie." She pulled at his hand until it cupped her breast. "I can't believe it's the popcorn that sticks in your mind."

Frank jerked his hand back. "You're right! She's not going to the drive-in."

Joan rolled over until she was face to face with Frank. "Not that I regret going to the drive-in with you." She kissed his lips. "Actually, it was kind of fun trying to keep your hands from going where they wanted to go."

Frank smiled. "And they still remember how to get there." He pressed up against her. "In fact." He nibbled a trail down the side of her neck. "I'm thinking they might want to visit some of those old places right about now."

Joan pulled back. "Old places?" She said louder than she needed to.

Frank felt an apologetic grin tug the corner of his mouth. "You know what I mean," he whispered as he closed the space between them and continued to plant hot kisses down her throat.

"Frank, do you think I'm old?"

He kissed his way up to her ear knowing when he arrived he had to be very careful with his words. But he didn't want to use words. He wanted to show her that she excited him just as much now as she did eighteen years ago when they were making out at the drive in movies. He smiled, cupped her face in his hands and put his mouth on hers.

Embers that had merely glowed in his gut jumped into flames. His kisses went from sweet to searing, and he gathered her close hoping to evoke the same feelings in her.

Joan pulled back. "Well do you?"

"No!" he yelled without meaning to.

"Shh!" She put a hand over his mouth, and they both held their breath for a moment. "Don't wake the kids," she whispered.

Frank reached up and pulled her hand away from his mouth to release a smile. "You're so young and beautiful, and I love you so," he said as he leaned forward to kiss her cheek. "So fill these lonely arms of mine, and kiss me tenderly." He kissed her other cheek. "And you'll be forever young and beautiful to me."

"Don't think I don't recognize one of Elvis Presley's songs when I hear it," she said with a playful slap on his shoulder.

"But it's how I feel," he said caressing her hip. "And Elvis said it so well."

Joan softly chuckled. "The least you could do is sing it to me."

"Dad!" a small voice came from down the hall. "I'm thirsty! Can I have some water?"

53

Frank sighed. "Why won't he get up to get a glass of water for himself?"

"He thinks the boogey man lives in the hallway."

"But we leave the light on. Doesn't Matt know by now that the boogey man can't withstand the light?"

"You say that as if you believe it, too."

Frank sighed and got out of bed. "I'll be right back, save my place for me." He shrugged on his robe and shuffled into the bathroom. Frank took a big gulp of water before refilling the glass for Matt.

Halfway down the hall, he found his bare feet grinding over the sharp points of a handful of jacks. "Aaah!" He hobbled around another group trying not to spill. How many times did he have to tell Susan not to leave them on the floor? As safety conscious as she was about household hazards, it was amazing how oblivious she was to her own carelessness. He shook his head and continued to Matt's room. He opened the door.

"Hi dad," Matt was propped up on his elbows squinting back the light.

"Hey sport," Frank said as he sat down on the edge of Matt's bed and handed him the glass. "Here's your water."

"Thanks," he said and brought the glass to his lips making sucking and gulping sounds as he drained half the glass. He handed the glass back. "I'm done."

"Matt?"

"Yeah dad?" He squirmed back under his covers.

"You know there's no such thing as the boogey man don't you?"

"Sure dad." He snuggled into his pillow and was

fast asleep before Frank could say another word. Frank set the glass on his nightstand and stepped lightly to the door.

On his way back through the hallway, Frank picked up the jacks and shook them in his hand. Susan would have to ask to get them back this time. He smiled. Maybe he would show her how to play marbles. They were a whole lot easier to step on barefooted. She wouldn't find a better teacher. Back in Indiana, he was Rolley-Hole champion for five years, and he would have stayed that way if one of the old Thompson brothers hadn't stolen his lucky Agate.

Frank stood at the bedroom door and scrubbed a hand over his jaw. He needed a shave. Joan hated beard stubble. For a moment he considered going back into the bathroom to shave. It would take the 'ouch' out of her grouch. He shrugged and shook his head when he realized it would take too long. No, he would just have to be careful.

A soft snore greeted him as he stood next to the bed. Joan was curled up in her usual sleeping position on her right side. Frank held the jacks a few inches above the nightstand and dropped them. They clattered loudly against the polished wood but Joan didn't stir. Not one little flinch.

Frank sighed and tossed his robe on the foot of the bed before crawling under the covers. He fidgeted, hoping to wake Joan from her coma. He traced his finger over the silhouette of her shoulder and watched her sleep. He fell back onto his pillow and waited until his disappointment subsided then drifted into a deep sleep.

# Chapter Seven

Shrill screams woke Frank, and he sat up as rigid as a tombstone.

"What is it?" he yelled as he threw his legs over the side of the bed and ran down the stairs taking two at a time.

Joan, Melinda and Susan were standing at the open front door. They screamed again in unison.

"Whoa, whoa, what's the matter?" Frank scowled.

"Look!" Susan pointed to something hanging on the outside of the door.

Frank blinked to clear the sleep from his eyes. He nudged them aside to get a look at what was upsetting them. He squinted and rubbed his eyes. He never saw anything like it. Who would do such a thing?

Gene shuffled in wearing his wrinkled kilt and shirt. "What's going on?" he asked as he kneaded knuckles into his eyes. His fine dark hair stood out all over his head resembling feathers floating this way and that as he walked.

"I was going to take the kids to school," Joan explained. "I opened the door, Matt ran out to get in the car and that's when I saw this!"

"Get rid of it, Daddy!" Susan cried.

"Okay sweetie," Frank said and gave her a hug. "It

will be gone when you get home from school." He smiled to reassure them. "Run along, all of you." He gave Joan a quick kiss on the cheek and guided her out by placing a hand on the small of her back.

Matt came running up the walkway to the porch. "What's taking you guys so long?" He stopped cold when his eyes focused on the front door.

"Neato!" he said as he cocked his head stared at it.

"Get back in the car," Joan said nervously. "Let's go now or we're going to be late."

Frank accompanied them out to the car and watched as they backed out of the driveway then drove away. He walked a few feet over to the Roberts' house. Nothing unusual. Just a single long-stemmed sunflower decorated the front door. He looked across the street at the MacCormack's', everything was in its place, quiet and serene. He shrugged and gazed down the row of pastel ranch style homes with manicured lawns and maple trees situated in the earth as carefully as acupuncture needles. This just didn't make sense he thought as he walked up the path of his own yellow house. Or did it?

Gene was examining the oddity. "Quite a piece of work isn't it?" he asked as he reached into his pocket for his glasses.

"I think I know who did this," Frank said with a faint curve curving up one corner of his mouth.

"Who?"

"Tito Tortuga," Frank said flatly.

Gene gave him a quirky look. "Sounds like an amusement park ride. What is a Tito Tortuga?"

"It's not a what..." Frank stepped up to the door.

"...it's a who. The guy I told you about last night."

"I'm going to throw on some clothes," Frank said. "We need to find someone who knows about this stuff."

"Where are we going to find someone like that?" Gene showed him a goofy smile.

"In the phone book, where else?"

Frank pulled the book down from the top of the refrigerator and set it on the counter. He rolled his eyes to the ceiling and frowned. What would he look under? He threw a look at Gene then wondered if it looked like the 'help me' look Matt had demonstrated for him.

"Will you put that thing in the trunk of your car while I look for a place?"

Gene snorted and strode up to take the phone book away from Frank. "Why don't you put it in the car while *I* look for a place?"

"Fine," Frank said and turned to walk to the door. He stopped. "What are you going to look under?"

"Never you mind, just let my fingers do the walking." Gene snagged his keys from the kitchen counter. "Put it in the trunk will you? I don't want that thing staring at me while I'm driving." He threw the keys, and Frank caught them one handed.

\* \* \*

A small bell tinkled as they opened the door of the shop. The sweet smell of incense surrounded them upon entering and the scent of perfumed candles mingled with it. Brass candleholders sparkled in the morning sunlight, and strings of colorful beads swayed as the outside breeze floated in.

"Are you sure we're in the right place?" Frank asked

as he glanced around at the shelves of books, candles, bottles of herbs and oils.

"May I help you?" A woman asked from behind the counter.

Frank and Gene jumped nervously. It was if she had just appeared there. She was middle aged, maybe forty. She wore a white peasant style blouse and a long earth tone skirt with a flower design. Her long black curly hair was neatly tucked under a white scarf pulled taut over her head and tied at the base of her skull.

"Uh, yes," Frank said and looked at Gene. "I have something here that I thought you might be able to tell me about." Frank set the article on the counter and looked at her.

She stared at it for a long moment then said, "Someone is very angry with you."

Frank gave her a patient smile. "Yes, that much I know. But what does this mean?"

"Someone has threatened you?" Her dark eyes flashed questioningly at Frank.

"Yes. He said, things may happen."

She grinned up at him. "His initials are T.T.?"

"Yes!" Frank exclaimed.

"Was he chewing on a root when said this?" she asked.

Frank winced and shot her a puzzled look. "A root? No. I don't know. He smashed a snail in my hand."

She threw her head back and laughed out loud.

Frank and Gene stared at each other then back at her. It took some time for her to compose herself.

"I can tell you that these things have begun to

happen," she said wiping a tear from her eye.

"Perhaps first you can explain what is so funny about this," Frank said struggling to contain his anger.

She became silent and stared intensely into his eyes. "You must learn not to take yourself so seriously," she finally said. "Celebrate the moments of your life."

"I'm sorry but when I'm awakened by my family's screams upon seeing this monstrosity hanging on the front door, celebration is the last thing that comes to mind."

"Maybe she doesn't know what it means," Gene said solemnly.

The woman smiled at Gene then disappeared through the rows of dangling beads into a back room. She came back carrying a small amber bottle.

"Put this on your rash, you will be back in your pants by tomorrow." She held the bottle out.

"What rash?" Gene asked looking at Frank.

She smiled warmly. "The crushed violets in the oil may even bring your lady friend back. That is if you will use it faithfully for seven weeks. Rub some on your gums, and you will find it very easy to wear your dentures."

Gene gazed curiously at the bottle. "What else is in it? Powdered lizard? Eye of Newt? Something poison?" He gingerly took the bottle from her fingers and held it up to the light. "Better things for better living through chemistry?"

"You will find no chemicals in that bottle. Only natural ingredients are in my healing oils." She took it back from him. "But...if you don't want it."

"I didn't say that." He snatched the bottle back and wiggled the cork out with the tips of his fingers. "How much do I owe you?" He waved the bottle under his nose and breathed in the heady scent.

"You come back and pay me after it works," she said.

Gene placed the cork back into the bottle and slid it into his shirt pocket. "What if it works and I forget to come back?" He gave her an impish smile.

She eyed him like a panther stalking its prey. "I guarantee you will not forget."

Frank huffed out a breath. "I'm happy that you have an answer for Gene, but what about this?"

The woman looked back at Frank and took several breaths. She closed her eyes and held out her hands with her palms up. "Put your hands in mine," she said softly.

Frank looked at Gene then slowly reached forward to rest his hands on top of hers.

Her eyes snapped open. "You keep your side of the street clean?"

"What?" Frank asked.

A serious expression came over her face. "You have done nothing to deserve this hex?"

"You think I deserve this?" He looked down at the counter.

The woman smiled knowingly. "Close your eyes."

It could have been Frank's imagination but it felt like her hands instantly warmed at least ten degrees. A tingling began at the center of his palms and swirled in clenching circles up his arms, over his shoulders and down his back. Her hands grew hotter and hotter until tiny beads of sweat began to form on his forehead. The back of his neck grew moist, and suddenly he wanted to turn and run. At the moment he thought he would have to break the connection, she spoke.

"You will need to collect the dirt from this man's footprint."

Frank pulled in a sharp breath and jerked his hands back. He swiped his forehead with the back of his hand and blinked.

He slowly released the breath. "What? The dirt from his footprint? How do I get that?"

She smiled and shrugged. "I always use a teaspoon." She turned and took a sack from the shelf. "This is my special mix of goofer dust."

"What's that?" Frank asked.

"A secret mix for a jinx crossing." She loosened the string that tied the top of the sack and opened it.

The pungent smell caused Frank to cough. He pinched his nostrils together.

"Once you mix this with the dirt from his footprint, he will have no choice but to leave town."

Frank gave her a skeptical look. "You want me to believe that some stinky powder mixed with dirt will make him leave town?" He shifted uncomfortably and looked up at the shelves. There were various sizes of sacks and bottles labeled respectively. 'Devil's shoestring, Mojo powder, Dragon's blood, Valerian root, alligator tooth'. There were three shelves full of them, and some of the names he wouldn't even try to pronounce.

"Yes, you must believe."

"What have you got to lose?" Gene asked.

The woman picked up the door hanging. "This is a very powerful curse," she warned and gave him a serious look. "A chicken was sacrificed, and its head was nailed to the wood." She traced the shape of the X in the center. "The feet were crossed below the head, just like a skull and crossbones." She looked up to make sure she had his attention. "All these snail shells are surrounding the image of death, laced together by the devil's shoestring root and sprinkled with the blood of the chicken." She rotated a splayed hand over the top of it.

Frank pursed his lips, and his eyebrows went up. "Yep."

"If you don't do something, you will experience a terrible fate." She shook her head sadly.

Frank's eyes widened, and he exchanged a fearful glance with Gene. "Like what?"

"You don't want to know but I will tell you that it will be worse than anything you could imagine, and it will last a very long time, maybe for the rest of your life."

# Chapter Eight

"She was interesting," Gene said as he drove them back to the house.

"I'll say. Are you going to use the oil she gave you?" Frank asked.

Gene had an uneasy expression. "I'm afraid not to." He looked pensive for a moment. "I hope it works, I'll be glad to get rid of this rash." He wriggled awkwardly in the seat.

"Who's going to do the honors?" Frank asked.

Gene looked puzzled. "What?"

"One of us has to collect the dirt from Tortuga's footprint." Frank held up a small packet of goofer dust. "And we have to get the rest of the things she named on this list."

"I'm the one with the car so I'll get the rest of the stuff," Gene said. "You get the dirt on him."

Frank nodded. "Just make sure," he said laying the list on the seat next to Gene.

"Make sure of what?" Gene asked.

"It's the real thing," Frank said.

"You don't have to worry about me," Gene assured him. "I listened to her instructions very carefully."

Frank stared out the window as they drove down the tree lined residential streets. They had lived in the neighborhood ever since Melinda was born. The trees along the parkway had flourished and matured from spindly saplings needing support from the fat rugged stakes lashed snugly at their sides to the thick branched renderings they were now, dusting the sky with their colorful broad leaves. Frank marveled at their strength, they were no longer in danger of snapping in the wind or being uprooted by a misguided bicycle. They had become the stability, the shade, the landmarks and the relationships in the neighborhood.

"I'm supposed to have that jingle done by the end of the week. I haven't worked on it at all." He heaved a sigh. "I just bought that new car payment, and now I have writer's block."

"What's it about?" Gene asked.

"Shoe polish."

"Why didn't you say something when we were back at the shop?" Gene questioned. "Maybe that magic woman has something to cure it."

"I've had writer's block before, I don't need magic. I need an idea."

They turned the corner to Frank's street, and Gene eased the car over to the curb to park. The front wheel climbed the curb then just as suddenly slipped back down causing the car to bounce in jerky response.

"There's Roberts' in front of his house," Frank said. "Honk your horn, I want to show him what his crazy gardener left on our door."

Gene tapped the horn, turned off the engine and hesitated before getting out. Frank couldn't get out of the car fast enough and was already half way up the path to

Roberts' door.

"Hey Rex," Frank said.

"Frank," Rex said without looking away from his prize rose bush. "Have you seen the blossoms on this thing?"

"No I haven't, but I'd like you to see something in my brother's trunk."

Rex looked at Gene's metallic mint green Chevy Impala curiously. He chuckled.

"You guys don't have a body in there do you?"

"Not a full one," Frank said snidely. "Just the few parts your gardener nailed to my door."

Rex's brows knitted. "What?" He looked around. "Tito? My Tito?"

"Yes your Tito," Frank repeated as he turned on a heel and started back toward the car. "We found it this morning. Almost scared Joan and the kids to death."

Gene opened the trunk as they approached and they all stared into it. No one spoke for several seconds, and the only sounds they heard were leaves rustling in the breeze, and the faint sound of the Helms' man blowing his horn a few streets over.

"Man, that's a lot of golf clubs," Rex said.

"What?" Frank said incredulously. "It was here! I put it here myself!" Frank snapped Gene a panicky look and began yanking the clubs from the trunk.

"Say, these are pretty nice drivers," Rex said as he fingered one of the clubs. "How much are you asking for them?"

Gene's chest puffed out. "They're twenty-five each."

Rex's eyes slid down Gene's front and stopped at the

wrinkled kilt. "Is this your line of work?" he asked then picked up one of the drivers.

"Not really, it's sort of a temporary side business right now."

Rex examined the club closely. "At that price, I'll take a couple of them."

Frank slapped Gene on the shoulder and pulled him aside. "You watched me put it in there didn't you?"

"Yeah I did."

"So, where is it?"

Gene shrugged and stepped back to Rex to complete the sale.

"I'll be on the golf course this afternoon," Rex said as he pulled the bills from his money clip and handed them to Gene. "We're teeing off at one." He leaned over the trunk and selected the two clubs he wanted. "I'm anxious to try these puppies out." He gave them a courtesy nod and turned to walk back to his house.

"You're gonna love those clubs. Pretty soon you won't leave home without 'em," Gene called after him.

Frank quickly followed Rex up the path. "Rex, speaking of puppies, would you mind keeping your dog in your yard? I caught her watering my front lawn three times last week."

Rex smiled. "Sure thing, Frank."

Frank turned then twisted back quickly. "And talk to that gardener of yours."

Rex waved a hand. "I'll tell him you said hello."

Gene closed the trunk and smiled. "Quickest sale I ever made." He pocketed the money and grinned again.

A trickle of cold rolled down Frank's spine. He

watched Rex get into his car and wave. It was apparent enough, Rex was toying with him. The depth to which he believed that took him by surprise. It also made him angry, very angry. Frank took an eager step forward to stop Rex from driving off, and then he remembered his unpleasant task. And as unpleasant as it seemed to be at the moment, if it worked, it would be well worth the money, time and trouble.

"I'm going to get the dirt," he said as he headed toward the front door.

"How are you going to be able to tell Tortuga's footprints from Roberts'?" Gene called after Frank.

"Maybe I'll get a little of both," Frank shouted over his shoulder. "You go get that other stuff, and don't mess up."

* * *

Frank had everything set up by the time Gene returned.

Gene stepped through the front door. "Jesus, Mary and Joseph," he said as he sat the cages he was carrying on the floor.

"We're going to fight fire with fire," Frank said as he poured a tablespoon of dirt onto a plain white saucer. "Does this look like a voodoo alter?"

Gene looked on in fascination. There was a board resting on two cinder blocks in the center of the room. Incense was burning, a black and white candle awaited a flame and a shot glass of salt sat between them.

"The ceramic turtle is a nice touch," Gene said as he stepped into the room.

"It was the closest thing to a snail that I could find,"

Frank said as he stood.

"Pee Caaah!" Came the deafening sound from one of the cages.

"What the heck is that?" Frank asked with both hands clamped over his ears.

Gene frowned. "It's the peacock I was supposed to get."

"Peacock?" Frank choked. "You were supposed to get a pheasant." He glared at Gene.

"They were all out but they promised me that pheasant and peacock are in the same family." Gene bent down to look inside the cage. He tapped on it gently and made a soft cooing sound.

"We're in the same family, too," Frank said loudly. "And look how different we are!"

Gene shoved an arm inside the bag he was carrying. He pulled out some tin foil, nails and parchment paper.

"Stop worrying; this isn't brain surgery you know."

Frank opened the book the woman had sold them. "It says we have to purify the magical tools."

"What are the magical tools?" Gene asked with growing excitement.

"This stuff!" Frank scowled and indicated the items on the board. "We have to sprinkle them with holy water."

"Where are we going to get holy water?" Gene asked.

"What?" Frank exclaimed. "You were supposed to get some. It's right there on the list." He pointed to Gene's pocket.

Gene looked confused. "Where?" He tugged the list

from his breast pocket and frowned at it.

Frank tossed the book on the couch. "I abbreviated it right there," he said while tapping the paper with his index finger. "B...C, Baptismal, Cleanse."

Gene looked at him with a critical eye. "I thought that meant 'black cat'." He reached down to pick up one of the cages. He brought it up to eye level and displayed a full-grown black cat crouching in the bottom of the cage. It hissed.

"Voila," Gene said.

"Weren't you listening when I was writing this stuff down?"

"I thought I was, but I didn't hear her say 'holy water'."

Frank snatched the book from the couch. "That's because she called it baptismal cleanse," he said as he huffed out a breath. "Okay, it says here in this book we can make our own holy water." He dashed into the kitchen and came back with a big brown plastic bowl half filled with water.

"What's that?" Gene asked.

One corner of Frank's mouth tipped up. "Tap water." Water splashed over the edge of the bowl and onto the alter as he sat it down.

Gene took the book from Frank's hand and read aloud. "All you need is a bowl of spring water and tablespoon of sea salt." Gene looked up. "Will tap water work? Is that sea salt?"

"Doesn't all salt come from the sea?" Frank asked.

Gene shrugged and watched as Frank measured what he thought was a tablespoon of salt into the bowl.

"Pee Caaah!"

Frank accidentally dropped the shot glass of salt into the bowl with a bloop sound. Water splashed out in all directions. He covered his ears. "How could such a small bird make such a big noise?"

The cat hissed then spit.

Frank snatched the book back. "Okay, now I'm supposed to hold my hands over the top of the bowl and visualize a white light flowing through them into the water." He handed the book back to Gene. "Here, you read the chant, and I'll direct the light."

Gene cleared his throat and gave Frank a quirky look. He wiggled like a golfer getting ready to tee off. He cleared his throat again and brought the book up.

"Come on," Frank snapped. "I only have so much light in these hands."

"Holy, holy water of life," Gene said then cleared his throat loudly. "May all it touches be cleansed right through?" He frowned. "That doesn't even rhyme. Aren't spells supposed to rhyme?"

"This isn't a spell," Frank said as he imagined squeezing out the last ray of light from his hands. He brushed them together and shook them at the top of the bowl. "Now we can cleanse the magical tools." He hesitated and looked down. "We need to cleanse the bird too, but first we need to enter a trancelike state."

"What kind of state?" Gene asked.

"We have to enter a trance by doing a skeleton dance," Frank insisted.

"Now that rhymes!" Gene cackled.

Frank straightened his spine and closed his eyes.

"Okay, imagine your skeleton."

"Wait! Nobody said anything about dancing," Gene complained. "Why don't *you* do the dance, and I'll do the trance."

"It doesn't work that way." Frank gave Gene a serious look. "Come on, we can't let some Brazilian gardener get the best of us."

"Okay," Gene said reluctantly then struck a ballet pose.

"Okay, start with imagining the bones in your toes and work your way up both legs at once. Flow into the pelvis." Frank began to rotate his pelvis in an Elvis Presley kind of way. "Shoot up the spine." His knees rose higher and higher with each kick. "Across the ribs and down the arms, up the neck to the skull and into the center of the brain." By the time he had finished guiding Gene into the dance, they were both spinning and jumping around the alter. With arms flailing and legs kicking, they imagined themselves great Voodoo priests unleashing their magical powers with the impressive force of a hurricane. Frank stopped long enough to light the candles then continued to dance like he was avoiding a floor full of fire ants.

Gene dipped his fingers in the bowl of water and bent down to open the door of the peacock cage enough to flick water on him. The foul took his chance and blasted like a missile out the door, flew three feet and landed on the couch.

"Pee Caaah!"

Suddenly the front door opened. Joan and the kids stood gaping and dumb struck upon seeing Frank and

Gene chasing the peacock around the room.

# Chapter Nine

Frank slowly unclenched, muscle by muscle. How could he know that dancing the skeleton dance and chasing a peacock would make him so sore? He yawned and rubbed knuckles into the corners of his eyes.

"Dad!" Matt stormed into the bedroom. "Are you awake?"

"I am now," Frank said.

"Did you see that bird yesterday?"

"I seem to recall chasing him around the house," Frank said as he rolled his head in circles to loosen the muscles in his neck. "Too bad we couldn't catch him."

"Uncle Gene got the closest to him." Matt stood up on the bed and flopped back down causing the bed to shake. "At least until he ran out the door and down the street." He stood again.

Frank reached up and pulled Matt down slowly. "Don't jump Matt, my back can't take it."

Matt giggled. "He just kept going and going and going…"

Frank smiled. "Yes, he certainly did."

"Pee Caaah!"

Frank and Matt looked at each other. "You hear that?" Frank asked.

"He's close," Matt said and got up to go to the

window. He pushed his pudgy fingers against the glass and left the print of his nose in the center of the pane. "Mom says to come down for breakfast."

Frank groaned. Orange juice, pancakes and a piping hot lecture coming up.

He threw on his robe and slid his feet into his fur-lined slippers. Matt thumped behind him one step at a time as he went down the stairs. By the time he reached the kitchen table he was one big nerve ending.

Frank stopped dead and could practically see the sparks generating from the electrical gaze Joan pinned on him.

"Morning," he mumbled then went to the cupboard to get a glass. He poured a half glass of orange juice and shuffled to the table to sit down.

Joan banged a plate of scrambled eggs and bacon in front of him. He watched the plate gyrate like a spun coin until it rested in silence a moment later.

"Isn't anyone else eating?" Frank asked looking around.

"We already ate," Joan announced as she poured a cup of coffee. She poured some half and half into the cup and set it in front of Frank.

"Thanks," he said avoiding her eyes. He thought of the Greek myth, Medusa, a terrifying character with snakes for hair and a fiery gaze. If you looked her in the eye, you would be turned to stone. He was beginning to wonder whether the notion of selling your soul to the Devil is more a metaphor than a real pact.

"How could you?" Joan finally said.

"Hmm?" Frank looked up innocently.

"You let your brother bring a farm animal into this house," she blamed.

"Joan," Frank said before putting on his most composed expression. "A peacock is hardly a farm animal."

"What were you doing with it anyway?" She waited for an answer with her knuckles pushed against her waist.

Frank stood and toyed with the tips of her shoes with his bare toes. "You look pretty this morning," he said cheerfully. "Did you do something different with your hair?" He smiled and playfully stroked her hair.

"Don't change the subject!" Joan glared.

Frank blew out a breath plopped back down into the chair. "Look, it was just a silly notion brought on by that Brazilian gardener."

"More like your crazy brother," Joan corrected.

"I *asked* him to help me," Frank explained. "It just got a little out of hand. We didn't expect the peacock to get out of his cage the way he did. And we didn't think he would run out the front door so quickly."

Joan shook her head and pursed her lips. "How late were you out last night?"

Frank took another swig of his orange juice. "We chased him until midnight then gave up."

Susan came to the table and stood next to Frank. "Daddy," she said with her customary official tone. "There's a man in a uniform at the door."

"A policeman?" he asked.

Susan frowned. "No, I don't think so. He looks more official than that."

Frank grimaced as he stood. He reached down and took the last swallow of his orange juice.

"Aaah, a day without orange juice is like a day without sunshine," he said as he made his way to the front door. Matt and Susan followed.

"May I help you?" he asked the visitor.

"My name is Frank Gillis from the department of animal control," he began.

"Hey! My name is Frank, too!"

The man stared at him with half-lidded eyes. "Some of your neighbors have reported that you have a peacock on the premises."

"That's absurd," Frank replied.

Susan stepped forward. "It escaped from our living room yesterday." She adjusted her hard hat after looking up at Frank. "Daddy and Uncle Gene were trying to teach it to dance."

Officer Gillis blinked at Frank. "This neighborhood is not zoned for these types of animals," he informed him. "I'm going to have to give you a citation. You will also need to relocate the fowl."

"I think he's already relocated himself," Frank said while running a hand down the back of his neck. "We haven't seen him since yesterday afternoon."

"Pee Caaah!"

They looked toward the sound to see the peacock standing peacefully on the front lawn. The iridescent blue-green sheen of his long neck sparkled in the sun as he pecked at the dichondra grass laden with morning dew. The officer turned back to give Frank a dubious stare.

"You have until this time tomorrow to relocate the bird." He ripped the top form from his citation pad and handed it to Frank. "See you tomorrow." He turned on his heel and walked to his truck.

Frank closed the door and turned to face Joan. Stone. The expression in her eyes could have melted iron.

"That's not the only thing you have to relocate," she finally said. "Gene let that dirty black cat out of his cage, and I'm sure he has fleas!" She pointed to the couch where Gene was sleeping with the cat curled up on his stomach.

"Dad?"

"Yes Matt."

"What's a fowl?"

Frank slipped an arm around Matt's shoulders. "Son," he began, "that can be a lot of things. It could be a violation in the rules of a particular sport, unfavorable weather conditions or something that's offensive to the senses." He flicked Joan a look. "But if you simply change the 'U' to a 'W' it becomes a bird."

"Was the man talking about our peacock when he said the word fowl?" Matt asked.

Frank patted Matt's shoulder. "I suppose he was."

"Can I stay home from school and help you catch him?" He looked up at Frank with a buoyant expression. His grin exposed his budding adult front teeth. "I can run faster than you can."

"Absolutely not, young man!" Joan said as she went to the coat closet to get her jacket.

Frank gave Matt an expression of agreement and shrugged.

"Your father has all the help he needs." Joan looked distastefully toward the couch.

"Now run to the kitchen, and get your lunch box or you'll be late for school." She shrugged on her jacket. "Susan, get your sister out of the bathroom, and get your things, we have to leave." Joan walked to the door then stopped suddenly as if an invisible shield dropped down from the ceiling. She turned to face Frank.

"I've invited some neighbors and friends for a barbeque on Friday night. I hope you'll have everything back to normal by then."

Frank's dark eyebrows met over his nose. "What?"

"In case you forgot, and I know you have, it's our sixteenth anniversary." Joan cocked her head and gave him a cheeky smile.

"I guess that's something you'll never know," he said defiantly and smiled back then leaned forward and kissed her cheek.

Of course he had forgotten. Somewhere between writer's block, entertaining his kilt-wearing brother and skeleton dancing to ward off black magic voodoo spells, the occasion had completely eluded him.

"Look Joan, couldn't we postpone our celebration for one week? The deadline for my ad is Friday, and you know what will happen if I don't meet it."

Joan opened the door and let the children file out. She removed Susan's hard hat as she passed and tossed it to Frank.

"Yes I do," she said and blew him a kiss. "That's why they call it a deadline Frank."

The door closed, and the house was nearly silent

except for the sound of Gene's particular brand of snoring. A long breath wheezed in, and then several short bursts went out of his toothless mouth propelling his lips to flap like the ragged door of a pup tent in the wind.

Frank stared at his brother. "Look Ma, no cavities," he mumbled to himself as he dropped Susan's hard hat and headed to the kitchen for a cup of coffee.

"Pee Caaah!" Came the sound from the side of the house.

Frank shook his head as he poured half and half into his coffee. He walked over and eased down onto one of the yellow vinyl kitchen chairs. It hissed dispassionately as air escaped from the cushion. Frank stared. His jingle was the farthest thing from his mind. Damn. The old idea of running away and joining the circus reared its ugly head once again. Which circus though? Barnum and Bailey wouldn't hire him without excellent circus skills so he would be forced to join a less reputable carnival troupe, one that he couldn't brag about. No, he was happy with who he was, a successful jingle writer. Jingle writers are clever, he thought, but they do not come up with a masterpiece all on their own. They take their cue from real life, and normally Frank had enough material to draw from right in his own back yard.

"Pee Caaah!"

Frank shot up from his chair and rushed to the closet. He squatted down and started tossing things out.

"Good morning," Gene said from behind.

Frank's head jerked around to see his brother's legs clad in pants, familiar looking ones.

"Hope you don't mind me borrowing a pair of your jeans." He patted the loose fitting waistline. "You got a belt?"

"Are you all out of kilts?" Frank asked sarcastically.

"Don't need 'em anymore." He beamed. "That woman was right, the rash is completely gone. Guess I'll be going back to pay her fee." He squatted down eye level with Frank. "What are you looking for?"

"A BB gun or something to anesthetize that peacock with."

"You mean we're not going to use him to ward off the voodoo spell?" Gene asked incredulously. "After we went to all this trouble?"

Frank stopped yanking things out of the closet and became quiet. "There was an officer here this morning from the department of animal control. I got a ticket and a warning to get rid of the bird by tomorrow."

The black cat jumped off the couch, sauntered over, rubbed his side along Frank's back and purred. Frank turned to look at him. "And that's another thing. You have to take that cat back to wherever you got him from. Joan doesn't want fleas in the house."

"I can't." Gene's face became grim. "If I take him back, they'll put him to sleep."

Gene gave Frank his best earnest look. "Take him back, dead. Keep him here, not dead."

Frank sighed. "Let me put it this way Gene." He sat back and put a hand on each knee. "Keep him here, I'm dead."

"Wait!" Gene's face brightened. "I have an idea!"

# Chapter Ten

Frank was buffing so hard, he didn't hear Matt come into the den.

"Dad."

Frank's head snapped up. "Oh, hi Matt."

"How do you spell relief?" Matt asked then suddenly noticed what Frank was doing. "Yuck, why are you spitting on your shoe?"

"It's called a spit shine son; I used to do this in the army."

Matt watched silently with interest. "Why don't you use shoe polish?"

Frank smiled and lifted the can of SP66 so Matt could see the culprit of his currently stymied ad campaign. "I'm just adding the missing ingredient."

"Can I help?" Matt asked as he bent to pick up the shoe from the floor.

"Sure," Frank said as he twisted around to get another cloth from his kit. Before he turned back, Matt had slowly licked half way up the side of the shoe on his way to the toe. Frank had to hold his breath to keep from laughing out loud.

"Betcha can't eat just one," he said handing Matt the soft cloth.

Matt's face held a sour expression as he smacked his

lips and ran his parched tongue over his lips. He smiled weakly and took the cloth from Frank.

"Now what did you ask? How to spell relief?" Frank asked. "Are you doing your spelling homework?" He spit on the toe of his shoe and buffed again.

Matt nodded, "Yep, my teacher says an idle mind is the devil's workplace." He held the shoe under his chin and spit forcefully. It shot over the toe and onto the carpet. Frank looked at him from the top of his eyes and smiled warmly. "Your teacher's right, but I thought it was idle hands being the devil's workshop." He rubbed the moisture into the rug with the toe of his sock. "My dad always said busy hands are happy hands."

Matt grinned and shrugged then he rubbed the shoe from side to side with the cloth.

"Mom said you and Uncle Gene were doing a voodoo spell, is that true?"

"Yes it's true," Susan interrupted. She was standing at the door, clipboard in hand with her back straightened in an authoritative stance. "It's all a myth you know," she said dramatically. "It's ridiculous to see modern intelligent people actually attempting to practice Voodoo sorcery to acquire personal power or turn someone into a walking dead zombie."

Frank frowned and shook his head. "I wasn't turning anyone into a walking dead zombie." Although it was a constructive suggestion definitely worth some added research. "It was sort of a ritual for protection," he explained.

Susan sighed and put her hard hat on. "My homework for tonight is to design an emergency evacuation plan for the family in case of fire." She held up the clipboard. Frank squinted at the crudely drawn map of the house with red arrows marking an escape route.

"Can we have a rehearsal after dinner?"

Frank spit on his shoe again and buffed. "Sure honey."

"Mom says dinner is ready." She spun around on her heel and walked away.

* * *

Frank cleared his throat as he sat down at the dining room table.

Joan glared at him as he spread his napkin over his lap.

"Where is your brother?"

"He won't be coming to dinner," Frank said and took a roll and passed the plate to Melinda.

"Where is Uncle Gene?" Matt asked looking around.

Frank put a slice of meat loaf on his plate. "I'm going to pick him up in the morning. Boy, this meat loaf smells great, I love Thursday." He felt Joan staring at him. He looked up. "What?"

"Where is he?"

Frank waved a hand. "It's a long story; we can talk about it later."

Forks and spoons tapped against the blue flower patterns of the dinner plates as they dished out roasted potatoes and carrots and buttered their rolls.

"Did you get rid of that bird?" Joan asked as she animatedly mashed her potatoes with the back of her fork. She tapped it loudly on the edge of her plate and

84

snatched the butter to slice a pat.

Frank wiped his mouth with his napkin and nodded as he swallowed a large bite of meat loaf. He looked down at his fork and swirled another bite around in a puddle of ketchup. "Yep. Gene devised an ingenious plan and snared him this afternoon."

"How did he do it?" Melinda asked before stirring her carrots and potatoes together.

Frank smiled. "Well, he used an old navy trick."

"You mean he made him walk the plank?" Matt chirped and grinned.

Frank reached over and patted Matt's head and chuckled. "No, not exactly."

"Did he dress up like a girl peacock and wink at him?" Susan asked with a laugh.

Frank grinned and looked around the table at them one by one. "Gene had the greatest idea," he said then sipped his water. He hitched his chair closer to the table. "He put a slice of bread in a dish and soaked it in gin." Frank tipped his head back and grinned at the ceiling. "Then he put the dish in the yard, and it wasn't long before that peacock came over to see what it was." He laughed out loud. "He gobbled it up like he hadn't eaten in a week. It only took a few minutes for that gin to start working on that old peacock, and before long he was exceptionally docile, and Gene just walked right over and picked him up." Frank emitted short bursts of laughter between wheezes.

Joan remained stone faced. "Isn't that how he met Helen?" Joan shook her head critically.

Frank stopped laughing abruptly. "I don't think

Helen likes bread."

"And the cat? Did he take that cat back?" she asked.

Frank cleared his throat and squished butter between two halves of his brown 'n serve roll. "That's what we need to talk about later," he said before chewing off a bite.

"All I want to know is if he got rid of that flea bitten cat," Joan replied with frustration.

Frank rubbed his mouth hard with his napkin. "Not yet. He's trying to find a home for him."

"So he's still here?"

"The cat is on the back porch. Gene's in the hospital."

"The hospital?" Joan's eyes widened.

"The doctor wanted to keep him one night to make sure he wouldn't develop an infection."

"Infection from what?" Melinda asked.

Frank squirmed in his chair. "I told Gene what you said this morning about the cat having fleas." Frank nodded at Joan. "He said he couldn't take the cat back to the shelter or it would be euthanized."

"What's that?" Matt asked innocently.

Melinda leaned toward Matt with a hard look in her eye, held her index finger up then made a throat cutting gesture. "Crreek."

Susan gasped. "Daddy, you're not going to let that happen are you?" Her hazel eyes bulged out with fear.

Frank held up a hand. "Don't worry, don't worry we'll find a home for Blackie before we let that happen."

"Blackie?" Joan sent him an admonishing glare. "How did Gene end up in the hospital anyway?"

"Cat scratches," Frank said in a low tone.

"Excuse me?" Joan dipped her head to establish eye contact with Frank.

Frank's shoulders slumped, and his head rolled back. "Okay, this afternoon Gene took the cat upstairs to give him a flea bath while I worked on my jingle."

Joan looked at him and cut him off in mid sentence. "Remind me to tell you something after you finish your Gene story."

Frank frowned a moment then continued. "Blood curdling screams snapped me out of my creative mode, and I ran upstairs to see what was wrong." His lips formed a hard line, and he shook his head slowly as he remembered. "Gene had decided that a bath would take too long, and he didn't want to get a ring around the tub so he undressed and took the cat into the shower with him."

It was the first time Frank noticed Joan smile all evening. His expression turned confused but he continued. "When I went into the bathroom, all I could hear was that cat throwing itself against the shower door over and over. He had turned Gene into a human claw post."

Joan threw her head back and laughed uncontrollably. Frank waited until she was somewhat composed before he went on. "I opened the shower door a crack, and that cat burst out like a wet bullet ricocheting off the walls all the way down the stairs."

Joan laughed louder and harder. She pounded her fist on the table and tapped her toes against the floor as if she were doing a dance. Silverware jingled and glasses jiggled. The kids stared at her with spellbound expressions on their faces.

"Joan, some of those scratches were very deep," Frank said seriously.

Joan laughed harder.

Frank huffed. "Anyway, I took Gene to the hospital to be treated for shock, and that's when the doctor said he wanted to keep him overnight."

Suddenly they heard the loud engine of a car pull up outside.

The kids ran, leaped on the couch by the front window and pulled back the curtains. It was an old yellow taxicab. They strained to see who was getting out of the back seat. By the time Frank and Joan walked to the window, Susan started to scream. It seemed to be contagious because Melinda and Matt began to scream, too.

"What is it?" Frank asked in a panicky voice.

"It's a walking dead zombie!" Susan pointed to a bandaged figure making its way up the path leading to the front door.

Frank pushed his face up to the window as the kids scrambled off the couch to get out of view of the trespasser. Frank remained silent watching the figure struggle up the path. Burglars didn't make their rounds in taxis did they? He looked back at the children huddled around Joan for protection. Mass hysteria was an interesting phenomena, he could practically see the vibrations of fright radiating from them. Frank felt a surge of adrenaline, the tightening of anticipation. He quickly went to the coat closet and grabbed Matt's baseball bat. He held it high above his right shoulder as he reached out for the doorknob with his left.

The door swung open, and the figure stood staring at him with fear struck eyes. Arms rose up in a defensive position. "No!"

Frank lowered the bat and stepped forward. He released a breath and smiled. "It's not a walking dead zombie, it's Uncle Gene."

Joan rushed forward. Her hands were clenched into fists causing her knuckles to turn a yellowish white. Frank dropped the bat, threw his arms around her and held her tight.

"I thought you were supposed to be at the hospital tonight," she growled.

Gene braced his body protectively. "I don't have medical insurance, and I didn't want Frank to get stuck with the bill. Besides, it's just a few scratches."

Joan's eyes slid down the myriad web of gauze wrappings. She shook her head.

"If you'll excuse me," Gene said as he sidestepped her. "I have to get back into my kilt."

They stood looking at one another. Frank seemed to be fighting a grin.

Joan's face had returned to stone. "I hope you were capable of returning to your creative mode after all of your escapades today and able to meet your deadline."

Frank shrugged. "Why?"

Joan wriggled from his arms and walked over and began clearing the dishes from the table. "I invited your boss to the barbeque tomorrow night."

# Chapter Eleven

Frank was glad he polished his shoes. It would be easier to tell his boss he didn't have the jingle ready if he could brag about the product. He tucked his powder blue polyester shirt into the waistband of his black slacks and gazed in the full-length mirror. He ran the tops of each shoe down the back of his pant legs and smoothed his hair. Not bad. But the moment of satisfaction was brief.

It came to pass, how could it not have? His worst fear. The day he would miss a deadline. The first time. He couldn't explain to his boss that he was battling black evil forces falling on him in the form of a Brazilian gardener. He walked to the window facing Robert's house and pulled back the curtain to check his backyard. He relaxed. There was no sign of Tito Tortuga today.

He could explain to his boss that he was caring for his injured brother though; there was certainly proof of that with Gene's skin snagged out like the threads of a cat clawed couch. He winced. That must have hurt like the devil.

Matt barged into the bedroom and jumped up on the bed. "Mom wants to know when you're coming down to help her." His voice jerked as he bounced up and down.

Frank slinked an arm around Matt's waist and wrestled him onto his back. "You go tell mom I'll be right there," he said as he tugged Matt off the bed and threw him up in the air and caught him. Matt giggled and hit the floor running. Frank straightened the bedspread and headed downstairs.

Joan was in the kitchen preparing the meat for the barbeque.

"Wow," Frank said as his eyes scanned the smorgasbord. "Is there any kind of meat you don't have?"

Joan flashed him a defensive look. "I want to make sure all of our guests are satisfied." She grunted as she cut a rib bone in half.

Frank stepped up behind her and put his arms around her waist. He bent and kissed the side of her neck then nibbled his way to her ear. He suddenly frowned. "What's that you're using?"

Joan hunched her shoulders and giggled as Frank continued to nibble. "I think your brother is trying to get on my good side. He gave me these rib cutters." She proudly held them up. "They look like pruning shears don't they?"

She demonstrated. "See?" She placed a rib between the blades and then pushed the handles together with a grunt. The rib fell in two pieces onto her cutting board. "Now it's easier to handle, and it looks like you have more meat."

Frank's face drained of color, and a tiny sweat mustache formed on his upper lip. "Did he give you a pair of large scissors, too?" he asked reluctantly.

"As a matter of fact he did," she said excitedly and turned to grab them from the counter. "These are perfect for cutting chicken breasts." She manipulated the handles making snipping sounds with the blades.

Frank sucked in a lungful of air. "Joan, you know how Gene likes to take samples of wares when he gets fired?"

Joan stiffened and nodded.

Frank looked nervously at the scissors and shears. "Well, did you know he used to work for the coroner's office?"

The scissors made a loud clatter when Joan dropped them on the floor. She stood frozen staring right through him. "How could he?" She looked around dazed and amazed. "I'm going to kill him!"

Frank reached out to put a hand on each of her shoulders. "He meant well, he just doesn't think sometimes."

"But," Joan's whole body protested.

"I'm sure they're clean," Frank continued. He smiled. "You thought I forgot didn't you?" he asked to quickly change the subject.

"Forgot what?" Joan looked confused.

"Happy Anniversary," Frank said and reached into his pocket. He pulled out a smell red velvet box and held it out.

Joan smiled and quickly turned to wipe her hands on a dishtowel. She turned back with tears brimming in her eyes. "Yes, I thought you forgot." She took the box and gave him a warm glance. She flipped the top open exposing a set of beautiful heart shaped diamond earrings.

"Oh Frank, they're absolutely beautiful." She leaned

forward and wrapped her arms around his neck. "A diamond is forever," she whispered in his ear then kissed him on the cheek and again on the lips.

Just like the payments, he thought. He placed a hand on each side of her face and gazed into her eyes. "I'm glad you're my wife and the mother of my children," Frank whispered and kissed her lips back.

"Nothin says lovin like something from the oven," Gene said as he came into the kitchen. He stopped abruptly. "Oops, didn't know this was a private moment."

Frank and Joan stared. Frank walked slowly toward Gene and made a complete circle around him.

"Where are they?" Frank asked.

"Who?" Gene's face wrinkled in puzzlement.

"The scratches." Frank lifted Gene's wrist and inspected his arm.

"Gone. Every last one of them," Gene said. "I used the oil that woman gave me, and it healed them right up."

"Great," Frank said as he dropped Gene's arm. His last excuse. Gone. Now he would have to tell his boss he was blocked and probably lose the account.

"Gene, why didn't you tell me these were trophies you collected from the coroner's office?" Joan's eyes blazed with anger as she held up the shears.

He waved a hand through the air. "Aw, they were hardly used. Maybe two autopsies, three at the most. No diseases, they were just murder victims. I cleaned them real good before I took them."

Joan's mouth dropped open. She turned clutching

her small velvet box and stomped out of the kitchen.

"She's mad isn't she?" Gene looked at Frank.

"You think?"

Frank faced off with Gene. "Look, if I need you to put your bandages back on would you do it?"

"Do I have to wear the kilt, too?"

Frank frowned. "No, I just need an excuse when my boss asks me why I don't have the jingle finished." He ran a hand over the side of his short-cropped hair. "If I tell him I was taking care of you, it will be more believable if you look like you've been injured."

Gene grinned and placed a hand on Frank's shoulder. "Frank you're not going to need that stupid job!" Gene turned to pace. "You know what we have here?" He dug the vial of oil from his pocket and held it up. "Pure gold!"

"I happen to like my job," Frank replied. "I have fun doing it, and most of the time I get it done when I'm supposed to."

Gene gave him an incredulous look. "You're not going to stand there and tell me you can't recognize a once in a lifetime opportunity when it's staring you right in the face are you?"

Frank looked over Gene's shoulder to see Tito Tortuga standing at the window on the side of the house. He flinched and yelled out in surprise. Gene's head snapped around.

"What is he doing so close to the house?" Frank asked as he rushed to the window and slid it open.

"Can I help you Mr. Tortuga?" he asked through the screen.

"I believe you have something that belongs to me," Tito said.

"No Mr. Tortuga, I do not have anything that belongs to you." Frank turned to look at Gene and shook his head.

"I think you have a piece of my shoe," he said in his Brazilian accent almost too thick to understand.

"I don't have any part of your shoe, and I would appreciate it if you would stay off my property."

Tito's stare was as sharp as a stiletto and seemed to carve him to the bone. "Pins of pain will bring you an ache in the head, you weel regret what you've done and said." He turned and left.

Frank watched until he was out of sight. There was something in the air, and it didn't feel right. He wondered if fighting voodoo with voodoo was the best course of action to take. After all, he and Gene were amateurs, fledglings of the black art next to Tito Tortuga, master of the deadly chicken head, snail shell wreath that they were yet to experience the results thereof.

"Call the woman at the shop," Frank said. "Things are getting worse."

Gene patted Frank on the back. "Don't worry. I went to pay her this morning. I hope you don't mind but I invited her to the barbeque."

"As long as she doesn't dress like a gypsy," Frank said. "What's her name anyway?"

Gene grinned. "It's Tilly."

"Tilly, what?"

Gene shrugged. "It doesn't matter." He placed a finger over the mouth of the vial and tipped it upside down. "If this stuff grows me some new teeth, we'll make a million bucks." He made a sour face as he rubbed the oil along the tough ridge of his gums.

* * *

The guests began arriving just as the coals in the barbeque were turning from ebony to ashy white. Frank raked them out evenly along the bottom of the barbeque with the tip of his fork. He was glad Joan had planned a barbeque. It gave him an escape from the obligatory conversations with neighbors and colleagues. He gazed through the sliding glass door as they began to drink and chat, showing each other snapshots of their families. He arranged the first layer of chicken onto the grill and brushed them with barbeque sauce.

Joan opened the sliding glass door and stepped out carrying a platter of marinated ribs. She sniffed at the fragrant smoke.

"I love to smell chicken on the barbeque, make sure you cook it thoroughly but not too long." She set the platter on a small table next to the barbeque.

"Don't worry about me," Frank said. "Everything is under control." He waved away the smoke as he turned several pieces.

Joan stood on her tiptoes to look over his shoulder. "I know how easy it is to cook the juice right out of it…"

Frank held up a hand. "It takes a tough man to make a tender chicken," he said with his best Clint Eastwood impression. "And I'm a tough man."

Joan giggled. She patted Frank on the shoulder. "Next time you go into the house, look towards your piano. You'll find your anniversary gift there."

Might he hope? Joan knew he wanted a new piano. Yes, the payments would be a struggle but it could be just the thing to vault him out of the slump he was in. He had been using the same old rundown upright for over ten years. Just the thought of sitting in front of the slanted lid of and baby grand sent a chill rolling down his spine.

They turned as the sliding glass door opened again. It was Joan Roberts. "Hello you two," she said as she approached. "It was so nice of you to invite Rex and me to your little barbeque."

"Are you kidding? We wouldn't think of having one without you," Joan gushed and stepped forward to give her a stiff hug.

"How nice," Joan Roberts said as she gazed back through the glass door at the large cluster of guests laughing and nibbling on cheese and crackers. "But, no one is here yet."

"Excuse me?" Joan said blinking around.

"I don't see any other members of the country club."

"We don't belong to the country club, Joan," Frank said as he slopped a spoonful of barbeque sauce onto several pieces of chicken. Billows of smoke belched out from the spattered coals. Frank fanned and coughed.

"Oh, I completely forgot that you didn't belong," Joan said curtly.

There was a short but uncomfortable silence before Frank asked, "Honey, would you mind making me a martini?" He nodded toward Joan Roberts. "Perhaps Joan could use a drink, too?"

Joan eyed him, then the barbeque. "It's a little early

for Martini's, how about a beer?"

Frank fanned at the smoke again. "Fine."

Matt squeezed through the door as Joan opened it. He ran out and stood silently watching as Frank basted and turned the chicken.

"Look dad, they plump when you cook 'em."

"Yeah" Frank said as he glared at Joan Roberts' backside as she walked back inside the house.

Joan returned shortly with another platter, this time it was steak kabobs. She set the platter down and handed Frank a bottle of beer.

"She had the nerve to tell me I used the wrong size macaroni in my salad." Heat flashed from her eyes, and she huffed out a breath. She brought her hands up and pressed her knuckles to her hips. "She's gone home to get a few folding chairs. She told me not to feel bad; she used to be very bad at planning parties, too." Joan snatched Frank's beer and took a long swig. "I think she could win an award for cramming the most insults into the least amount of time." She took another gulp and handed the bottle back. "If they had such an award that is." The heels of her sandals pounded the flagstone as she stomped her way back into the house.

Frank looked in and noticed that his boss had arrived carrying a bottle of wine. He watched as he gazed around the room wearing an expectant smile. He probably thought Frank had met his deadline. Now what?

"Matt? Go in and close the drapes for me will you?"

"But then no one can see you barbeque," Matt replied.

"Exactly."

Just before the drapes met in the middle of the sliding glass door, Frank got a glimpse of Tilly talking to Gene, and he waved his tongs to get her attention.

# Chapter Twelve

"You have any luck with the jinx crossing?"

Frank turned to see Tilly standing behind him. He didn't see her come through the door, and he hadn't heard any footsteps.

He pinched a chicken leg with the tongs and turned the meat his shoulders hunched to dispel an unpleasant feeling from the back of his neck. "I don't think we performed the ritual correctly," Frank said.

"The book I sold you had specific instructions, step by step," Tilly said with a coldness in her voice.

Frank glanced up from the grill. "We didn't have the right bird but the dance and the trance went well, we just didn't count on being interrupted."

Tilly strolled out to the edge of the lawn and stooped down to poke at the grass. "Did you mix the dust with a spoonful of dirt from his footprint? Then did you sprinkle it where he will walk?"

"Yes," Frank replied quickly. "But…"

"But what Mr. Beal?" She turned and glowered at him.

Frank pointed at her. "There! That's the look he gave me this morning. I think he knows what we're up to."

Tilly nodded knowingly. "That is the evil eye, and you must act quickly to banish it."

"Oh no," Frank held up a hand. "No more voodoo magic around here. I don't believe in the stuff."

"Tell me Mr. Beal, do you believe in this?" She stepped over to him carrying something in her hand. "Your grass is covered in them."

Frank gazed down in disbelief at the snail she held in the palm of her hand. He rushed over to the aquarium and pulled off the tarp. It was empty, and every last bit of foliage was dryer than desert sand.

His forehead wrinkled in puzzlement. "What?" He searched madly for an escape hole. "How did they get out?" He ran to the lawn to see hundreds of snails languidly eating his grass.

"Now do you believe?" Tilly asked as she swiped her hands together, and the snail disappeared from her palm. "You are very fortunate. Like a good neighbor, Tilly is there. I can help you."

Frank dashed back to the barbeque. Flames had begun to blaze up fueled by the grease dripping from the grill. He cussed as he sprayed at them with water from a plastic bottle. He waved an arm and choked back the smoke but it was Tilly's air of mystery that smothered him more than the smoke from the barbeque. He piled the meat onto the two platters that Joan had left. The green was for chicken, and the blue was for the steak kabobs. Or was it the other way around?

Tilly proudly placed a charm around his neck. It was a bone of some kind threaded onto a leather band. She smiled. "This will bring you luck and help you to banish the evil eye."

Frank sighed and stared at her. "If only it would

help break my creative block," he said wistfully. He stacked the last bit of smoking chicken onto the platter.

"First you must enter a mild trance," Tilly instructed.

Frank smiled and held up his beer. "Working on it." He drained what was left in the bottle.

"Then you must look around your house through slightly squinted eyes. If you see black specks flitting in the air, it is negativity sent from the evil eye." Tilly's dark eyes widened, and she nodded wisely. "You must light a stick of incense and waft the smoke around them while you say this...*In the name of the powerful spirits, I bid you black specks of evil to begone! Never to return!* Be sure to end the chant with a powerful scream."

Frank took a step back, his left eyebrow rose in cynicism. He shook his head and picked up the platters and went into the kitchen through the back door. No way. He chuckled to himself. He was done with this crazy hoodoo stuff. But, out of curiosity, he squinted his eyes upon entering the house. Not only were there dark specks floating in the air but also there were chubby indefinable figures mingling around with the guests. Frank stood surprised and frozen in his squinty-eyed stance.

"I'll take that," Joan said and took the kabob platter and walked it to the dining room table.

Suddenly as if he planned it, without fear or intention, Frank raised the smoking chicken platter above his head. "In the name of the powerful spirits, I bid you black specks of evil to begone!" He walked forward and waved the chicken platter around the room, smoke curled from the charred pile of dead offerings as guests gazed curiously at him. He stopped and turned. "Never to return!" He stood face to face with his boss. The powerful scream he was instructed to let out sounded more like a rusty bedspring.

"Mr. Gladstone," Frank stuttered. He lowered the platter in front of him. "Care for a piece of chicken?" He cleared his throat.

"I have to say Frank," he gingerly removed a leg from the smoking pile and placed it on his plate. "One of the hardest parts of running an advertising firm is dealing with eccentric employees." A slow grin spread across his face then out of the blue he threw his head back and laughed a deep belly laugh.

Frank smiled and shrugged. "We do chicken right."

Gladstone took a bite of the chicken and licked at his fingers. "The only thing I'm interested in you doing right is the SP66 shoe polish jingle," he said as he reached for the napkin he was holding under his arm and scrubbed it across his lips. "I hope you'll be playing that for me today."

"Uh, right sir." Frank turned to take the chicken back to the table. "Be right back," he said over his shoulder.

"Frank!" Joan rasped into his ear. "What the heck is going on with you?"

He shrugged and gazed around the room then made his way, weaving through the tangle of guests in the living room to the corner where Tilly stood.

"I commanded the evil specks to go," he said as he approached. "Is that what was blocking my creativity?"

Tilly squinted her eyes and looked towards the middle of the room. "I still see some. Did you use the incense I told you to use?"

"I used a smoking dead chicken," Frank said.

Tilly shook her head. "How do you expect the magic to work if you can't follow the simple instructions that I give to you?"

"Will you make them go away? I just want everything to be perfect. Get rid of this block, and I'll do anything, I'll pay you what ever you want."

"Of course you will pay me," Tilly said with a serious stare. "How do you think I pay my bills? With mojo tonic?" She placed a hand on Frank's shoulder then felt her way up the side of his neck and finally placed her hand on the top of his head. "This is worse than I thought; a very high level of hexing." She cocked her head and waved a hand in front of the charm around his neck. "You need to sit over there." She pointed toward his piano. "The best seat in the house for healing this ailment. I will say a magic chant that will make your wish come true. Now go." She pushed him in the direction of his piano.

Frank walked to his instrument with great reluctance. What if he couldn't play at all? He looked down to see his hands were shaking. He didn't have the slightest idea of a shoe polish jingle. He stopped suddenly and gazed at his piano. It wasn't a baby grand but the same old Sherman Clay upright. Not even a new bench.

"I made it myself," Joan said from behind. "I know how much time you spend on it."

His old bench had been covered with a thick cushion decorated with the design of the family crest. The colors were royal blue and red and depicted two knights face to face.

"Is it rude to sit on the family crest?" Frank asked as he lowered himself on the bench.

"You've been sitting on it for years," Joan said with an impish smile.

"Thanks hon." He said as he bounced gently on the cushion. "I love it."

He cautiously placed his fingers on the keys and softly struck a minor chord. He tipped his head back and closed his eyes and began playing a smooth a rendition of 'Smoke gets in Your Eyes.'

Applause came from the guests as they wandered toward him. He ended the song with a flourish of notes then smiled and looked around. His boss was approaching. Frank immediately segued into a torchy version of 'At Last.'

"That was for my wife," Frank said upon finishing. "For our sixteenth anniversary."

Another round of applause filled the room.

"Do you take requests?" Mr. Gladstone asked over the clapping.

Frank smiled and nodded in tempo with the next song, 'Route 66'. He smiled when he saw Matt pushing through the crowd to stand proudly next to him. Following a long introduction, words suddenly began to take form in his mind, and before he knew it he was singing them.

*'If you ever plan to look your best,*
*Use the polish that beats all the rest,*

*Get your kicks SP66*
*They'll shine heel to toe all the way,*
*Shoes look bright all night and every day,*
*Get your kicks SP66*
*Now you go through a mud hole,*
*Scuffin up your arch sole,*
*And don'tcha know that loafer looks mighty gritty*
*You'll see*
*Dirty insteps*
*That always forget to shine*
*Give yourself a shoeshine; buff them till they look fine,*
*Brown ones, black ones even navy blue kind.*
*Why don't you get hip to this wing type tip?*
*And get the polish that's slick, cool and hip,*
*Get your kicks SP66*
*Lickety spit SP66*
*Get your kicks SP66*
*Lickety spit SP66'*

Mr. Gladstone slapped his forehead following a long and passionate applause.

"My God Frank, a parody, I love it! This isn't just a radio jingle. I can envision television commercials, too!" His fleshy cheeks jiggled as he patted Frank hard on the shoulder. "What's more, I know our client is going to love it."

The timing of Tilly's chant couldn't have been better. And while Frank was as grateful as anyone could be, he hoped she wouldn't charge him too much for her services. He knew she wasn't an idiot. She was fully aware of the miracle she had just performed. He glanced over to see her face beaming with satisfaction. What the heck? He would pay her whatever she asked. It was worth having the anvil of deadline pressure off his shoulders.

Matt lightly tapped a finger on Frank's shoulder. "You got that idea from me didn't you dad? Especially the lickety spit part." He grinned, and Frank could see a youthful version of himself mirrored back innocent and uncomplicated.

"Yeah Matt, I guess I did."

# Chapter Thirteen

Frank awoke to the smell of fresh coffee and bacon. A slow smile claimed his face. Joan hadn't cooked breakfast on Saturday for months. He rolled onto his back and listened. Silence. The kids must be out with their friends, he couldn't hear the usual weekend bickering.

The party had been a big success, the guests were well fed, and they had a good time. Gladstone was happy with his jingle. All that mumbo jumbo and Tilly's good luck bone charm had really paid off. He reached over and took it from his nightstand. He turned it between his fingers and gazed at it in the morning sunlight. He tried to imagine what type of bone it was. It was small, only a couple of inches long. He turned it sideways. Cow? He dangled it from its leather strap. Chicken? It swung from side to side like a miniature pendulum. Shark? Suddenly a dark thought crossed his mind. It couldn't be. He put it back on the nightstand and sat up. He shook his head as he threw his legs over the edge of the bed. No, it wasn't a human bone. At least he refused to think it was.

He was shocked upon entering the kitchen. Melinda was frying the bacon and buttering a stack of wheat toast.

"Hi, Daddy, how do you want your eggs?"

"Melinda," he stuttered. "I didn't know you could

cook?"

'Oh, Daddy, just because I haven't done it doesn't mean I don't know how." She giggled. Her face was freshly washed free of all make-up tweaks and tricks and in her navy blue jeans and peasant top, she remarkably resembled his little girl again.

"Where is your mom?"

Melinda looked up from the toast and shrugged. "I think she's out working in the yard."

"In the yard?" Frank's expression flashed from bewildered to fearful. "Oh no!" He ran to the back door and swung it open. Joan was on her way in carrying a mixed bouquet of perennials and roses.

"Good morning my darling husband," she said cheerfully. She was wearing a pair of his jeans with large cuffs rolled up to her shins. The plaid flannel shirt gave her a country appearance, and she looked as beautiful and youthful as Melinda.

"Where have you been?" he asked nervously.

Joan frowned and turned to look behind her. "Just out to the yard, why?"

"Did you go to the side of the house where the Roberts' live?"

Joan gave him a peculiar look. "Don't worry, they sleep in on Saturday," she said and took a vase from the top of the refrigerator. She dusted it with a dishtowel. "Did you see their new Cadillac convertible? It's absolutely beautiful."

"Do you feel okay?" Frank asked with panic rising in his voice. "Any headache? Shortness of breath? Fainting spells? Deafness? Blindness? Paralysis?" He took the vase from her hand and set it on the counter. With a hand on each of her shoulders he looked intently into her eyes. "Did you walk along the hedges where the properties meet? Let me see the soles of your shoes, do they have powder on them?"

Joan smiled sweetly and kissed him on the cheek. "Get out of your robe Frank, it's making you paranoid." She picked up the vase and ran some water.

"Were there a lot of snails in our yard?" Frank asked.

"None that I could see, would you mind asking Susan and Matt to come to breakfast?"

"Where are they?"

She smiled at him over her shoulder. "In the living room watching television."

"Daddy, how do you want your eggs?" Melinda asked again.

"Just make me a squishy sandwich," Frank replied and dashed toward the living room. As quiet as it was, one of them had to be bound and gagged or at least dead. He braced himself for the worst. He froze when he reached the living room. There they were, sitting quietly on the couch watching cartoons.

"What's going on in here?" he asked suspiciously.

"Hi, Daddy," Susan said cheerfully. She handed Matt the television guide. "Here, Matt, it's your turn to pick what we watch."

"That's okay, Suse. I like what you pick," Matt said and handed the guide back.

Frank was speechless. It was as if someone had kidnapped his family during the night and replaced them all with, well...perfect people. His imagination unspooled with terrifying images of Tito Tortuga carrying them off in gunnysacks one by one into the dark night then replacing them with impeccable duplicates.

"Come to breakfast," Frank whispered.

Immediately Susan and Matt slipped from the couch, turned off the television and walked toward the kitchen.

It comforted Frank somewhat that they remembered the usual seating arrangement at the dining room table. Melinda brought a plate full of bacon. Joan followed with a stack of warm toast and a bowl of fluffy scrambled eggs.

"Here's your squishy, Daddy, just the way you like it," Melinda said as she set his plate in front of him. He watched her as she sat in the chair next to Joan, the one she had been sitting in for the last thirteen years.

"Do you want to say grace or shall I?" Joan asked Frank.

Frank sat down, a look of confusion permanently tattooed on his face. "Be my guest," he replied and bowed his head.

"Lord," Joan began, "bless this meal for which we are about to receive, through your bounty, Christ our Lord."

Frank raised his head and gazed at his family with their heads still bowed.

"But most of all dear Lord," Joan continued.

Frank's head dropped again.

"Thank you for the wonderful man who provides this family with the security and comfort that can only come from fathomless love and devotion. He is a wonderful husband and dedicated father, and we are grateful to have him in our lives."

"Amen," they said in unison.

Frank looked up into his family's smiling faces and felt a guilty shudder. Had he caused this? In his selfish quest to outdo the Roberts' had he conjured up some devil-spawned evil? A mysterious enchantment that ensnared his chaotic home and turned it into a place of gratitude and serenity? Talk about high level hexing.

For a moment the only sounds he focused on were bowls and plates being passed around the table politely with courteous responses.

An odd look washed over Joan's face as she stared past Frank. Susan and Matt screamed.

Frank's head snapped around to see Gene standing in the kitchen doorway. There was something different about him but he couldn't put his finger on it. He was wearing regular clothes in place of the family Tartan kilt, which put Frank more at ease. Gene produced another broad smile. Frank gasped, the children screamed again, and Joan stood in preparation to run.

"What the matter with you?" Gene asked. "You're acting like you've never seen me before." He shook his head and scooted a chair up to the table between Joan and Frank.

"Yes, but it's you're..." Joan said as she pointed to his face and slowly sat back down.

"I know, I know, you've never seen me wear my teeth." He clicked his teeth together making snapping sounds and held his face in a grimace. He laughed. "I decided to keep them in a more conspicuous place."

"You mean in your mouth rather than your pocket?"

Frank asked.

"Exactly," Gene said as he spread jam on a slice of toast. He glanced over at Frank. "So, are you convinced yet?"

Frank's eyebrows knitted. "Convinced?"

Gene elbowed his arm. "Yeah, the new business I was talking to you about yesterday." He lowered his voice. "Maybe that oil didn't grow a new set of teeth but it sure as heck made it comfortable enough for me to wear the false ones."

"I don't know Gene; I have to think about it."

Gene shook his head with a look of disbelief then took a large bite of his strawberry jam toast.

"How's your squishy, Daddy?" Melinda asked.

"What the heck is a squishy?" Gene asked.

Frank held up his sandwich. Several strips of bacon and an egg over easy. He took a bite and the yolk drooled onto his plate. He swabbed it up with and extra piece of toast.

"Outstanding! Just like your mom makes," Frank replied with a drip of yolk trickling down his chin.

"What a mess," Gene said. "It's disgusting."

Frank smiled. "If it doesn't get all over the place, it doesn't belong in your face," he said as he scrubbed his chin with his napkin. He took another bite and the yolk spilled over the top of his sandwich onto his fingers. "M'm, M'm, good."

Melinda watched him eat her sandwich with an expression of gratification. "Of course it tastes like Mom's, I learned to cook by watching her. And I know all about her secret ingredient."

"What's that?" Susan asked.

"All you add is love," Melinda grinned and looked at Joan.

Joan smiled back warmly and rubbed Melinda's back. "Thank you honey."

Frank shot to his feet. He threw his napkin on his plate. "That's enough! I don't know what you're all up to, but it's scaring the bejeebers out of me." Frank turned to Matt. "Since when do you and Susan agree on anything? Why aren't you laughing hysterically and spitting out your milk?" He paused. "And Susan, where's your hard hat?" He pointed to her neatly combed hair. "You haven't given me any kind of a violation warning this morning, aren't you concerned about the family's safety anymore?" Frank looked around at them with a sort of frantic expression the same one James Stewart had in 'It's a Wonderful Life' when no one in his hometown knew who he was. "Melinda, where are those painted on raccoon eyes I'm so used to looking into?" His eyes assumed a suspicious squint. "Why are you cooking?" He reached down and snatched a glass of water from the table and drank it quickly as the water poured down the corners of his mouth. He coughed and wiped his mouth with the sleeve of his robe. He hoped his harsh words were jarring them back into their true character. "And Joan, what's all this business about working in the yard? Liking the Roberts' new car? And what's with all the praying for Gods sake?" He waited for answers in the prickly silence that followed.

Gene reached up and patted him soothingly on the arm.

"Frank please stop, you're scaring the children," Joan said with tears in her eyes.

# Chapter Fourteen

"What are you doing?"

Frank watched as Gene stood on the top step of a six-foot folding ladder.

"I'm doing what Tilly told me to do," Gene explained. "For added insurance."

"What kind of insurance can a bunch of bananas provide?" Frank asked.

Gene looked down over his shoulder. "How can you question these things after all you've seen?" He turned back and tied a black ribbon around the stems and hung them from the roof of the house. "There," he said with a nod. He stepped down, each step squeaking from the ache of his weight as the ladder quivered.

Frank shaded his eyes with his hand as he gazed up at the swinging fruit. "How long do they have to stay up there?"

"Till they rot," Gene said. "Then we have to take them to a crossroads and bury them."

Frank frowned. "What? Do you have any idea what rotten bananas smell like?"

Gene grinned extremely big to show off his set of teeth. "Yeah but they will absorb any residue of the evil eye in the house."

"Speaking of evil eye, what am I going to do about

my family's odd behavior?" Frank asked.

"The only odd behavior I noticed this morning was coming from you," Gene said as he folded up the ladder and balanced it on top of his shoulder. "Are you wearing that charm Tilly gave you? She said it would calm you down."

"Calm *me* down?" Frank exclaimed.

The front door opened and Susan and Matt stepped out onto the porch. "Daddy, can we go to the carnival in the parking lot of the Piggly Wiggly?" Susan asked.

"You want to go to the carnival?" Frank asked Susan.

She nodded.

"With Matt?"

She nodded again.

"Matt, you want to go to the carnival with your sister?"

Matt smiled and slipped his hand into Susan's. "Yep."

Frank flashed a *see what I mean* glance at Gene then reached into his pocket. "Here's five dollars, make sure you're back before dinner."

Susan plucked the bill from his fingers. "Thanks Daddy, and don't worry, I'll take good care of my little brother," she said as she slipped an arm around Matt's shoulders and used it to guide him down the street.

"There." Frank pointed after them. "That's the odd behavior I'm talking about."

"That's not odd, it's nice," Gene said as he headed toward the garage. "I'm going to look for a job; I'll be back for dinner."

Frank stared stupidly as Gene got into his car and drove off. He ambled to the door gazing at the still swinging bananas hanging from the roof. Where would they find a suitable crossroads to bury the rotten bunch? Wasn't the crossroads where Robert Johnson sold his soul to the devil in exchange for guitar expertise? Frank stopped. Is that what the SP66 jingle was? The Devil's music? Frank shook his head. No, Johnson came from Mississippi. This was California, what could the devil possibly want in California?

Melinda opened the door and bounced out. "Bobby and I are going to the movies, Daddy."

"Be home for dinner," Frank mumbled.

Frank stepped inside the house and closed the door. He leaned against it, head tilted back with his eyes closed. Was all this really happening? Crazy. That was another possibility. He sensed it coming closer. Closer. It was like a ominous dark cloud floating over his head ready to burst open and rain more crazy all over him.

His eyes snapped open when he heard faint music coming from the upstairs. He held his breath to hear better and tried to make out the song. He slowly moved towards the staircase and took three steps up and stopped. The music was a little more audible, but he still couldn't make out what it was. Cautiously he continued up the stairs at a snail's pace. At the top of the stairs he could hear the song plainly coming from his bedroom. It was Etta James singing 'At Last'. He began to hum along with it, he didn't know how not to.

The image that greeted him behind the bedroom door was one that would burn in his memory forever.

"At last, my love has come along," Joan said seductively as he entered.

Frank stared, mouth agape with eyes widened. A vast number of feelings quickly swept through him ranging from paralyzing fear then weaving over and around confusion, lust, pride, concern for his personal safety, making a complete three sixty and ending up rendering him immobile.

"What's the matter darling? Cat got your tongue?" Joan was wearing a black satin and lace bustier corset complete with garters, black silk stockings and high heels. The bustier appeared to be a couple of sizes too small, which would explain why so much of her was threatening to spill over the top. She was holding a long black cigarette holder that embraced the filter of an unlit cigarette. Frank's eyes scanned her auburn hair falling loosely around her shoulders, a stunning change from the French twist she usually wore.

Frank found himself madly dueling between an absurdly Victorian response to toss his robe over her to cover her up and a stronger primitive response that ordered him to seize this voluptuous woman in his arms and ravage her.

"I love the way you're looking at me right now," Joan said in a low sensual voice, "it's been a long time since we've had the chance to be alone." She moved slowly toward him rubbing her hand down her thigh then back up again. Frank's eyes followed her hand over the curve of her hips then inched up her front, paused to rest then rose to her scarlet lips parted slightly divulging the tip of her tongue glossing languidly across her top lip.

Frank shuddered. He hadn't had butterflies in his stomach for a long time although these felt more like bats.

"Did the kids go to the carnival?" she asked softly as she reached out and slid her hands across his chest before slipping them under his robe.

Frank nodded anxiously.

"And Melinda went off to the movies?"

Frank leaned his head back and exhaled a trembling breath as Joan pushed his robe off his shoulders and let it drop to the floor.

"Yes," he whispered. He was powerless to move a single muscle. Frank began to take in shallow breaths when he felt her lips brush across his cheek and settle softly on his lips. Instantly every nerve in his body responded with the desire and longing that had seemed to have disappeared from their relationship. Desire that had become lost in the countless responsibilities and chores that took precedence over what they had deemed low priority activities.

Frank's face tingled everywhere her lips touched, hot and moist. She fastened her mouth to his throat, nibbled then kissed her way down the front of his chest as she unbuttoned his pajama top. Frank's heart battered a fierce rhythm against his sternum causing his upper torso to vibrate against her lips. He felt her fingers slide up to massage his shoulders then she pushed the top of his pajamas off his bare shoulders until it joined his robe on the floor. She slipped her arms around his waist and crushed him to her breasts.

"Are you ready to unveil the torch of cupid?" she asked lustfully between kisses.

Frank was so excited at hearing her words; he barely heard the doorbell ring. His arms found their way around her, and he quickly lowered his head to feel his lips against her perfumed throat.

"Frank, someone is at the door," Joan whispered between gasps.

He kissed her again; he was having way too much fun to stop. "They'll go away," he said as he continued to run his fingers through her hair and nuzzle his nose against her ear.

"What if it's one of the kids? They could be locked out," Joan said as she nudged him back.

Frank sighed and reluctantly stopped kissing Joan. Great. Just his luck. The first nooner he's been offered in years and someone comes to the door. He squeezed her hand and turned allowing his hand to slide through hers until their fingertips separated.

The doorbell rang again when he was halfway down the stairs.

"I'm coming," he called gruffly. "Keep your pants on." At that moment he realized he was only wearing his pajama bottoms. He gripped the banister as he slid down the last three steps on the heel of his foot.

Frank stood behind the door and opened it wide enough to see who was standing on the porch. "Oh, Mr. Gillis. Can I help you?" Frank's voice cracked.

His official voice was louder than it needed to be. "I am here to follow up on the Peacock incident."

Peacock incident? He made it sound as if it were

some high-level espionage set up by the government.

"Why yes," Frank said and opened the door a little more. "The incident has been resolved, and I'm happy to report the bird was returned to its former residence which by the way, is zoned correctly for, as you put it, these types of animals."

Gillis's eyes floated from Frank's face to his neck and down his torso. He cracked a smile and shoved his clipboard forward. "Would you please sign this?" He grinned at Frank. "It's your statement saying that the bird has been removed from the premises."

Frank's expression went from restlessness to annoyance. He took the pen and scribbled his signature. He thwacked the pen down on top of the form. "There you go, and thanks for making our neighborhood a safer place to live in"

Gillis chuckled. "You bet Mr. Beal, you have a fine afternoon."

Frank watched him step off the porch and frowned when he saw Gillis throw his head back and laugh out loud.

After closing the door and double locking it, Frank ran into the downstairs bathroom to brush his teeth and put on some of that stinky cologne Joan bought him last Christmas. It didn't do a thing for him but seemed to crank her up to lover level status. He could only wonder what it would do to her when she was already in red-hot lover mode.

The moment he gazed into the mirror, he realized what Gillis had been laughing about. There were red lipstick prints patterning his forehead, cheeks and lips.

The imprints marched all the way down his front and stopped just north of the border, the elastic on his pajama bottoms. He blushed for a moment then shrugged and brushed his teeth then patted on the cologne careful not to disturb Joan's lip prints.

He took the stairs two at a time back up to the bedroom. He was running for the border.

# Chapter Fifteen

"What are you doing out here?"

Frank rose from his crouched position from behind boxes of Christmas ornaments and turned to see Gene standing behind him.

"The garage the only place that I can hide from Joan, she's afraid of spiders," Frank said. "She attacks me whenever we're alone." He rubbed a hand on the side of his neck. "She's not herself. I haven't played the piano for days."

"Shame on you for acting like this," Gene snapped. "What man wouldn't give his right arm for a woman who shows you love the way Joan does?"

"I think I was happier when I wondered whether or not she loved me." Frank yanked the waistband of his pants out. "Look! I've lost ten pounds. I think she's trying to kill me with love."

Gene crooked an elbow around Frank's neck and patted his chest. "Come on Goofus, I'll protect you from the big bad sex fiend." He walked him toward the house.

"I think I need to pay Tilly another visit and find out why this stuff is happening."

Gene frowned. "What stuff?"

"All this perfection is frightening me."

"Maybe you just need a good psychiatrist," Gene

said smiling.

Frank shook his head. "No psychiatrist in the world would believe what's been going on here. It's driving me nuts."

"Isn't that a requirement for seeing a psychiatrist? Being nuts?" Gene patted Frank on the back.

"Look, I didn't say I was nuts, I said this is driving me nuts. The truth is, sometimes I feel like a nut, sometimes I don't."

"When don't you feel like a nut?" Gene asked.

Frank didn't answer.

Joan met them at the front door in her red satin embroidered robe. It was a gift from her bride's maid but Joan hadn't worn it since their wedding night. She smiled at Frank with half lidded eyes and stepped forward so he would have to brush up against her as he stepped through the door. Frank knew what was underneath her robe. He shuddered at the memory of the black satin and lace bustier corset, and Joan's dance of Salome while taking it off. He had to admit her dance had improved but the thought of tangling with her one more time today made his shoulders slouch with exhaustion.

"Gene's going to go with me on an errand," Frank said as he tried to untwine Joan's arms from his neck.

"Can't it wait?" Joan ran her fingers up the back of his head causing his hair to stand on end. "I need you to help me with something." She pressed against him, kissed his cheek and nuzzled his neck.

"No, I don't think so." Frank turned his head toward Gene who was looking on wearing a goofy grin.

"I have urgent business to take care of," Frank said

stepping back from Joan.

She closed the space between them. "I have urgent business, too. Don't you want to take care of me first?" she whispered in his ear.

"I'm going to have to give you a rain check," Frank said with an uncomfortable smile. He gave her a friendly kiss on the forehead.

"But it isn't raining," Joan complained.

"Yes, well you see this rain check is only redeemable when it *is* raining," Frank explained and turned to push Gene out the door.

"You're right," Gene said as they walked to the driveway. "You *are* nuts."

\* \* \*

Tilly was wearing a similar peasant style blouse and ankle length skirt that she wore the first time they came to her shop. She smiled broadly from behind the counter when they walked through the door.

"Ah yes, and how are my part-time voodoo priests?"

Gene shrugged. "Great!"

Frank gave him a heated glance. "Great for him, but not so great for me." He placed his palms on the counter and sighed heavily. "Tilly, I need your help."

"Of course you do." She smiled and cocked her head. "What do you need?"

"Something has happened to my family," Frank said ruefully.

"Did you lose them?"

Frank look startled. "No." His expression softened. "Well, not physically. They're still there. They just aren't being themselves, including this one." He thumbed over his shoulder toward Gene.

Gene flashed back a bewildered look.

Tilly smiled serenely. "How are they different?"

"Well," Frank began then paused and scratched his head. "They're too perfect."

Tilly's eyes sparked with surprise. "But that's what you wanted! You asked for it from your own lips."

Protest bathed Frank's face. "I never said I wanted them to be perfect."

"But you did Mr. Beal. At your barbeque when your boss was pressing you on your deadline. You asked me to rid the house of evil eye and that you wanted things to be perfect." She nodded her head once. "Your house is now free of evil eye, and everything is perfect, isn't it?"

"That's not what I meant though; I only wanted the day to go perfectly."

Tilly slowly tipped her head back. "I see." She leaned forward; her dark eyes captured his with a penetrating stare. "So you were not specific enough for Tilly to use the correct spell were you?"

"Apparently not." He rubbed his hand over a three day beard.

"So now you want me to perform an uncrossing spell?"

Frank shrugged. "I just want them to be the way they were."

Tilly nodded. "What would you be willing to pay?"

"Just tell me what it costs, I'll pay."

Tilly smiled sympathetically. "Everyone is willing to pay for what they want, even before they know the price. Don't you know that payments can go on forever?" Her look became solemn. "The price can be wide and cut clear to your soul."

"Is that your price? My soul?"

"Mister Beal," Tilly said patiently, "I am not the devil. What would I do with your soul?"

Frank shrugged. "What does the devil do with them?"

Tilly chuckled and stepped back to one of the shelves behind her. She ran a finger slowly along the ledge. "Here we go." She took a small bottle from the shelf then continued to remove two more then returned to the counter. One by one she held them up.

"This is uncrossing oil, you will use nine drops." She pushed a pencil and a pad toward him. "You better write this down."

Frank took the pencil and squinted at the label on the vial. "Nine drops, got it." He looked up, anxious for the rest of the recipe.

Tilly nodded. "This is Rosemary oil. Put seven drops in a glass of rainwater."

Frank's head snapped up. "Rainwater! Where am I going to get rainwater?" He swallowed hard, and his left eye began to twitch wildly. "It isn't going to rain is it?"

"Are you afraid of the rain?"

Gene laughed. "He's afraid of rain checks."

Tilly reached underneath the counter. "I have rainwater." She shook her head, and her face twisted in a scowl. "I have to think of everything. It's a good thing in California that when it rains, it pours." She set a lidded jar of murky looking water in front of him. "Once you have added the Rosemary oil and Uncrossing oil to the rainwater blend it thoroughly."

"Blend thoroughly," Frank repeated as he scribbled.

"As you do that, you repeat this chant, *Break this hex, give it the boot, free my life from this evil spell.*"

"There it is again!" Gene chimed in. "That's what's wrong with these spells, they just don't rhyme. Isn't a powerful spell supposed to rhyme?"

Tilly glared at him. "Do you want your rash back?"

Gene held up a palm and stepped back in silence.

"Then you must place this mixture in a window for three days."

"What?" Frank stared. "This is going to take three days? I thought it would work right away like your evil eye remedy."

Tilly sighed. "Mr. Beal, you're not that powerful. You must cast spells the slow way."

"Okay then, you come to my house and cleanse the curse." Frank's eyebrows rose in a hopeful expression. "Okay?"

Tilly shook her head. "No, it is best that you do this one yourself."

"I was afraid you'd say that."

"On the fourth day, sprinkle several drops of the water in all the corners of your house making sure no one sees you do it."

"You can bet your sweet bippy no one will see me do it," Frank quipped as he wrote.

My rule of thumb is I never bet anything sweet," Tilly said.

Frank looked up with a silly smile. "Good rule of thumb."

Next Tilly held up a small burlap pouch in each hand. "After you have sprinkled the water in the house, take a bath every day for seven consecutive days, adding a teaspoon of Uncrossing Bath," she held it up, "and Jinx Removing powder."

"What do I do when I'm in the tub?" Frank asked.

Tilly shrugged. "I don't know, why don't you sing?"

"What words should I sing?"

Tilly frowned. "You're the jingle writer Mr. Beal."

"Right." Frank blushed. "How much do I owe you?"

"Twenty-five dollars."

"What?" Gene exclaimed. "He's getting all this for twenty-five, and you charged me fifty dollars for one little vial of oil?"'

Tilly looked at Gene as if she were staring through a pane of glass. "*Itchy itchy, burn, burn until you shut your mouth you'll earn.*"

Gene's hips started swaying in a sort of Elvis Presley kind of way. "Ow!" He winced and wriggled. "Okay, okay!" He pressed his hands together as if he were praying. "Sorry." He began to madly scratch the inside of his right leg.

"How's that for a rhyme?" Tilly threw her head back and laughed. "I hope you have some of that oil left." She bagged Frank's order and pushed it across the counter.

"Thanks Tilly," Frank said softly and turned to leave.

"Mr. Beal," Tilly said.

Frank stopped and turned to look at her.

"You will have some ingredients left over when you are through."

130

"What should I do with them? Bury them at a crossroads?"

Tilly slowly shook her head. "Put them in an aquarium with a few gallons of water. You have an aquarium don't you?"

"As a matter of fact, I do," Frank said looking at his feet. "What should I do with the water?"

Tilly gave him a bowled over look. "Fish Mr. Beal, put fish in it."

Frank nodded agreeably.

"By the way, have you had anymore trouble with your neighbor's gardener?" Tilly asked.

Frank looked at Gene then scratched his head. "You know, I haven't seen him for days."

Tilly smiled. "Foot track magic never fails."

# Chapter Sixteen

"*Break this hex, give it the boot,*" Frank sang as he sprinkled water mixture around the corners of the living room, "*free my life from this evil spell.*"

"Honey, what's this?" Joan asked.

Frank spun around and swung the jar behind his back. "I thought you went grocery shopping. What are you doing back so soon?"

"I haven't left yet silly, I couldn't leave without giving you a good-bye kiss."

"Oh, right." Frank leaned forward offering only his puckered lips making sure Joan wouldn't touch any other part of his body. He cracked an eye when she didn't kiss him immediately.

"What's this?" she asked again as she handed him the folded paperwork. "A strange man just delivered it."

With the water hidden behind his back, Frank took the papers and opened them one handed. "What?!" He dropped the jar of water on the carpet with a thud. Half of its contents spilled before he could retrieve it.

"What's that?" Joan asked as she peered over his shoulder.

"Nothing," Frank stuttered as he put the paper under his arm screwed on the lid to the jar and set it on the floor. "Just a little rain water and room fragrance."

He walked quickly to the front door and stepped out onto the porch. With a hand shading his eyes he looked up to the roof.

"Damn!"

"What is it Frank?"

"Roberts," Frank said as he slowly turned to face the Robert's house. "He's suing us for personal injury." He squinted back the sun as he looked again at the documents. "It says he suffered substantial back injury from slipping on a bunch of bananas that were lying on our walk."

"Bananas?" Joan looked confused. "That's ridiculous. Why would we have bananas on the walkway?"

Frank flashed her a guilty look. In the next moment, his eyes narrowed, and his face hardened. "Fine, if he wants to fight, I'll give him one," he said stomping into the house straight to the closet.

"What are you going to do?" Joan asked from behind.

Frank stopped tossing things out of the closet and looked back over his shoulder. "What do you mean what am I going to do? I'm getting my tennis racquet. I'm going to fight fire with fire." His timing couldn't have been worse. Not only was his racquet missing but also he suddenly remembered that his cache of snails had vanished mysteriously.

"Well, let me know if you find a lawyer attached to that racquet of yours," Joan snapped and walked out slamming the door behind her.

A slow smile spread across Frank's face. It was the

first real sarcastic thing Joan had said in many long days. The slamming door was music to his ears. Tilly's uncrossing spell was beginning to work already. Frank dashed back into the living room and grabbed the jar of rainwater. He danced around sprinkling the corners. *"Break this hex, give it the boot, free my life from this evil spell,"* he chanted as he pranced. *"Break this hex, give it the boot, free my life from this evil spell,"* he continued as he trotted up the stairs sprinkling the fragrant water as he went.

The front door swung open. It was Gene.

"Where have you been?" Frank asked. "I have a bone to pick with you about those bananas you hung from the roof."

Gene huffed and waved a hand. "I buried them."

Frank's voice wobbled as he came down the stairs. "Roberts is claiming that he slipped on them and hurt his back." He pointed toward the front of the house. "Right there on my walkway."

Gene frowned. "I wondered about that. I had to scrape them off the cement. They weren't even rotten yet, hadn't even gotten out of the speckled stage."

"Well it's a good thing," Frank said. "He'd probably sue me for that, too."

"What was he doing on your walkway?"

"How the heck would I know?" Frank waved a hand expressively. "He probably whacked the bananas down with one of those golf clubs you sold him and slipped on them intentionally."

Gene rubbed his chin thoughtfully. "You know? That's not a bad idea." He smiled. "You could probably make a pretty good living that way."

"Yeah right, I don't think you'd find enough bananas hanging from people's roofs to have a steady flow of income. I guess I need to get a lawyer."

Gene waved the idea away. "Nah, just let your homeowner's insurance handle it."

"Are you sure?" Frank asked.

"That's what you pay the premiums for isn't it?"

Frank stiffened. Sure, why not? In sixteen years, he had never filed a claim. He nodded thoughtfully. It felt good knowing that in the worst case scenario, if the house and its contents were destroyed, they would at least have some money in their pockets to start over with. Law suits were tricky though, sometimes judges favored the plaintiff.

* * *

"Welcome to Seasonal Insurance Mr. Beal," the agent said with a hand extended. Frank took hold and shook it noticing it was as soft as a chamois and clammy. Frank absently rubbed his hand down the leg of his pants as he sat down in the chair across from him.

"Ulf Russo." His pudgy cheeks blushed. "Sorry," he said as he nodded toward Frank's hand. "My doctor says my Sympathetic Nervous System is overactive. I sweat a little too much. Did you know that two thirds of our body's sweat glands are in our hands alone?"

Frank cleared his throat. "Why no, I didn't."

"And you are?"

"I'm his brother."

"Please sit," he said indicating the chair next to Frank. A long silence followed as Russo sat and folded his hands on his desk in front of him. His smile was so wide Frank could fairly see flashes of light glittering off his polished teeth. A legal pad was placed on the desk in front of him next to a sleek gold plated pen.

"How can I help you today?"

"I'd like to file a claim," Frank said as he gazed around at mahogany book shelves filled with leather bound books and lustrous walls adorned with gold framed oil paintings depicting the sights of Paris and Rome.

"I see," Russo said without picking up his pen. "Can you explain the nature of the claim?"

"My neighbor hurt his back when he fell on my walkway."

Russo's eyes narrowed. The black leather of his office chair squeaked as he leaned back and laced his fingers behind his head.

"Does your neighbor have any witnesses to his injury?"

Frank looked at Gene then back at Russo. "I don't know. We were only notified this morning that we are being sued."

Russo was silent as he stared at the ceiling. Slowly, his mouth curved up to one side. He leaned forward and pressed an intercom button.

"Miss Henry, would you bring me Mr. Beal's policy information?"

"Yes sir," came a muted response.

Russo's mouth twisted from side to side like he was chewing the inside of his cheeks. "The first thing we have to do is check your liability coverage." He leaned forward and folded his hands.

Frank's insides clenched at being under silent regard. "Ulf," he said looking at Russo's ebony desk plaque. "That's an unusual name."

Russo smiled. "It's Swedish."

"Russo sounds Italian," Gene said.

"My mother is Swedish." He pointed toward the bookcase to a mahogany framed photo of an elderly woman with short hair worn in a finger curled twenties fashion. "She insisted that I carry her father's first name, Ulf. My son's name is Ulf, too."

He must be giddy with pride, Frank thought. "Does it mean something?"

"Wolf," Russo said with a pompous smile.

The office door swung open and a slender woman came in carrying a manila file. She smiled pleasantly at Frank and Gene as she placed it on Russo's desk then quickly left the room.

"Thank you, Miss Henry," Russo said almost inaudibly and waited for her to close the door before he opened the dossier. "Let's have a look." He took in a breath and whistled its release. "The liability portion of your policy will pay for both the cost of defending you in court and any court awards."

Frank relaxed and felt his back melt into the curve of his chair. He smiled and gave Gene a wink.

"However," Russo said as he looked up. "It only pays to the limit of your policy."

Frank's composure slipped a rung. "What does that mean?"

"Tell me something," Russo said as he re-laced his

hands behind his head. He hitched a leg up and rested his ankle on his knee. "How did the accident happen?"

"Well," Frank began. "He claims that he slipped on some bananas."

Russo stared. "And these bananas, how did they get on your walkway?"

"That's just the thing, they weren't on the walkway. They were hanging from the roof."

Russo frowned, uncrossed his legs and picked up his pen. "Most folks hang wind chimes."

"Yes, that's true but my brother thought it was a type of good luck charm."

Russo's head snapped up. "Your brother hung them?"

"It's sort of a religious gesture that offers a home and everyone in it protection."

Russo smiled and shook his head. "I know bananas are a good source of potassium but I've never heard of them offering any sort of protection."

"I was helping to avert the evil eye," Gene chimed in.

Frank flashed him a glance that said to put a sock in it.

"Mr. Beal, you should contact me before doing any home improvement projects..." he stopped in mid sentence and frowned. "What is the evil eye?"

"It's the glance of doom," Gene offered. "You wouldn't believe what we went through with the skeleton dance and the peacock." Gene hitched his chair forward until he could place his elbows on the desk. "The evil eye brings bad luck on people, and if anybody had bad luck, Frank did." He jerked his chin in Frank's direction. "Black specks were floating around in his house like sparkles in a snow globe."

Frank elbowed Gene's ribs and smiled. "Sometimes my brother gets carried away."

Russo smiled dryly. "Do you expect me to believe that Mr. Beal had bad luck because someone looked at him the wrong way?"

Gene scowled. "You want to see my rash?"

Russo sighed and leaned forward. "Here's the bottom line. You have a five thousand dollar deductible for any injury your neighbor sustained from these...bananas." He glanced at Gene. "But I seriously doubt that your policy would cover any damage caused by a..." Russo rubbed his chin. "Are you a visiting relative?" he asked Gene.

Gene nodded.

"By a visiting relative." He shrugged and slapped the folder shut. "I would recommend that you upgrade your liability limits and lower your deductible. Your premiums will be more but from what your brother is saying, I recommend a no-fault medical coverage." He clicked his sleek gold pen and few times then leaned back.

"If I do that, will it cover this claim?" Frank asked.

Russo cleared his throat and leaned forward again. "No, but at least you will have peace of mind for the future. I would suggest talking to your neighbor and try to negotiate a settlement."

Frank and Gene stood. "Thanks for your time," Frank said without offering to shake Russo's hand again.

Russo nodded and stood. "Here at Seasonal Insurance, we try harder."

* * *

"Overactive sympathetic nervous system, my foot!" Frank ranted as they walked through the parking lot. "He doesn't have a sympathetic nerve in his body!"

"Why don't you let me talk to Roberts? It's the least I can do to help. After all, I was the one who hung the bananas," Gene said.

Frank gave him a sidelong glance. "What? And explain things the way you did in there?" He thumbed back at the office building behind them. "I don't need that kind of help thank you very much."

Gene looked at him with a mixture of hurt and surprise. "Then I think we should stop off at Tilly's on the way home."

# Chapter Seventeen

"Back so soon?" Tilly smiled as they walked up to the counter of her shop. "How is your family doing? Back to normal?"

"I think I detected signs of life this morning." Frank looked sheepish. "In my wife anyway."

"Very good Mr. Beal." Tilly's eyes flashed. "It doesn't take long for the uncrossing oil to work."

"There's a different problem now," Gene said as he propped an elbow on the counter then cradled his chin in his hand. "You told me to hang a bunch of bananas to bounce any bad luck back to Roberts."

"Yes-s," Tilly said with a hiss that sounded snake-like.

"Well, I hung them, and it seems they fell down, and Robert's slipped on them and hurt his back." He slapped his hand down on the counter and shook his head. "Now he's suing Frank for his injuries."

Tilly threw her head back and laughed out loud. "It sounds like..." Tilly struggled to say between snorts, "...the bananas are working just fine."

Frank raised a palm. "Wait, how can they be working if he's suing me?"

Tilly stopped laughing as suddenly as she started. "Tell me," she said looking at Gene. "Did you light the black candles and burn the repelling incense?"

Gene rubbed a hand on the back of his neck. "No, I forgot."

"And did you utter the chant I told you while hanging them with the black ribbon?"

Gene's face brightened. "I did use black ribbon," he said proudly. He frowned. "But I didn't say the chant. I couldn't remember all the words. I think I could have remembered them if they rhymed."

"How can you expect results to be favorable when you don't follow the instructions?" Tilly shook her head slowly. "This is a serious ancient art Mr. Beal. It is nothing to play with. Half measures avail you nothing. It is like tipping the first domino, each action will produce a consequence, and if it is done incorrectly, the consequences can be disastrous."

Frank sighed deeply. "I'm beginning to believe that."

Tilly's face melted into a compassionate expression. "Okay Mr. Beal, I will help you one last time."

Frank's smile appeared truly grateful. "Thanks Tilly," he said softly.

Tilly reached under the counter and slowly brought up a red flannel pouch. She placed it on the counter as delicately as if she were handling an active bomb. She looked at them with her black eyes blazing then reached under the counter again. This time she had a bowl of liquid in her hands. She placed it next to the pouch and held her hands over both.

Frank started to reach for the pouch. "What do I do with this?"

"No!" Tilly yelled causing him to jerk his hand back.

"This magic is only for Tilly. You never had it, never will." She closed her eyes. Her lips moved to form words but there was no sound.

Frank and Gene looked at each other and shrugged.

After what seemed like minutes, Tilly opened her eyes. They were no longer deep and black but looked like mirrors reflecting back their images.

Frank gasped and took a step back.

"Come forward!" Tilly commanded. "Both of you, and close your eyes."

Frank and Gene took shaky steps forward until they felt the edge of the counter.

"Now press your cheeks together!" she commanded.

They turned back to back and closed their eyes.

"Not those cheeks! Put your faces together!"

They chuckled a moment then stood side by side and pressed their faces together.

"Lower," Tilly's voice was thick, and she seemed to have an accent now.

They bent their knees and waited for further instructions.

"Lower!" Tilly ordered. "Put your chins on the counter."

Frank wanted to open his eyes to make sure no one else was in the shop. He couldn't imagine what anyone would think if they saw him and Gene bending over the counter, hands laced behind their backs, faces stuck together, resting on their chins. He wanted to open them but he couldn't.

Tilly dipped her fingers into the bowl and swirled them around while uttering her chant, *"bitter, hour, vinegar-B! Keep the sickness off of thee!"*

"I like it when they rhyme," Gene whispered.

Frank elbowed him to keep quiet.

Tilly drew her fingers from the liquid and flicked the solution into their faces three times.

They squeezed their eyes shut and grimaced as they felt the drops spray their faces. Frank started to bring his hand up to wipe the moisture away.

"Don't move!" Tilly demanded.

Frank froze.

Then Tilly opened the red pouch and poured out a handful of dust that was the color of violets. *"Spirit of healing, bring blessings upon Frank and Gene, may wealth, health and good fortune be forever theirs."* She held her dust filled palm to her lips and blew forcefully.

In the next moment, Frank and Gene were standing outside beside Gene's car. They opened their eyes and blinked at each other. With bewilderment lining their expressions, they gazed around.

Gene began laughing. "Your face, it's purple," he said pointing at Frank's face.

"So's yours," Frank said as he wiped the inside of his sleeve down his face.

"It's not coming off," Gene laughed and pointed again.

Frank looked toward Tilly's shop but it had vanished, and in its place was a tamale stand. Frank slowly walked toward a man wearing a large sombrero who was busy making tamales.

"Excuse me," Frank said.

"You want a bueno tamale?" the man asked. "They

are outstanding and they are mild," he said in a Latin accent.

"Where's Tilly?" Gene asked.

The man slowly raised his head to expose his face.

"Tito Tortuga!" Frank exclaimed.

"Hello Mr. Beal, how are you today?"

"What are you doing here?" Frank asked. "And where is Tilly?"

Tito smiled. "I have to earn a living, like every other man."

Frank gazed around at the area. "I thought you were a gardener."

"I do lots of things, so does Tilly."

"You know Tilly?" Gene asked.

Tito smiled again and held up a tamale. "You want one?"

"We better get going," Frank said and pulled Gene by the arm.

"It's a good thing I am not a one-eyed, one horned, flying purple people eater," Tito called after them then burst into raucous laughter.

Gene eased the car away from the curb clutching the wheel until his knuckles were white. He gave Frank a wide eyed look. "Wow!"

"Turn around," Frank yelped after they had driven a couple of blocks. He looked through the back window of the car. "Turn around," he said excitedly. "There has to be some explanation for this."

"Okay, give me a chance," Gene said and signaled his intention. He turned into a driveway that led to an alley and headed back in the direction they came in. He drove slowly along the back entrances of the shops along the alley then pulled up to the corner where Tilly's shop once was. It was gone. Tilly was gone. Tito was gone, too.

Frank looked at Gene with confusion and stared out the windows. "What the heck?"

Gene looked around and swallowed hard. "We're at a crossroad."

\* \* \*

Frank took a few deep breaths to appear composed. He opened the front door and was met by an argument between Susan and Matt.

"Daddy, tell Matt he can't hog the television all day," Susan whined and adjusted her hard hat to sit squarely on her head.

Frank smiled broadly. "Matt, take turns with your sister," he said as he ran up the stairs. He slowed down when he reached the master bedroom. Every muscle tensed at the prospect of being ambushed by Joan in her black satin and lace corset. He stopped and listened. The sound of crying came from Melinda's bedroom. He knocked gently on her door and opened it a crack.

"Melinda? You okay?"

"Oh good, you're back," Joan said. She was fully dressed in her favorite flowered house dress. With knuckles on hips, she glared down at Melinda on the bed. "You need to talk to your daughter."

Melinda looked up at him with a tear stained face. "She's acting like she found drugs in my drawer," she wailed.

Joan bent down and snatched something from the bed. She marched toward Frank causing him to take a step back.

"Just look at this!" She held it out.

Frank released a relieved breath and frowned. "What is it?"

Joan's eyes were drawn to Melinda. "Tell your father what this is."

"Oh, Daddy, it's just a harmless voodoo doll that Bobby's Aunt Tilly gave to me. She said it would bring good luck to the family and eliminate the evil eye."

"This evil eye business has got to stop," Frank blustered. All of a sudden he paused and stared at her. "Bobby's Aunt Tilly?"

Melinda nodded then made a few involuntary hiccups. "His mother's sister." Melinda continued to cry softly. "She and Uncle Tito were visiting from Brazil," she managed to say. "Mr. Roberts hired him to be his gardener while they were here."

Frank fingered the doll then sniffed at it. It smelled of cloves and cinnamon. He walked forward and sat on the edge of the bed. He placed a hand on Melinda's back and spoke quietly, "sweetheart, voodoo is a serious ancient art. It is nothing to play with. It can have disastrous results if you don't know what you're doing."

"Not to mention, good Christians *do not* practice voodoo!" Joan added.

Frank waved a hand to calm Joan.

"One look at my face will prove my point," Frank said and leaned down to tilt his head toward Melinda. "See what the power of voodoo can do?"

Melinda's head popped up. Her nose was pink and swollen. Her cheeks were blotchy, and her lips had lost their definition as a result of her weeping session. She gazed at him and frowned. "What's wrong with your face, Daddy?"

"It's purple!"

The corners of Melinda's lips curved up slightly. "No it's not."

Frank surged up and dashed to the mirror. The purple residue was all gone. He turned his head from side to side. Only a heavy five o'clock shadow blurred his features.

"It was purple an hour ago right after Tilly blew dust in our faces."

"You know Tilly?" Melinda asked with growing interest. She sat up and pushed her legs over the side of the bed.

"We met a couple of times," Frank said as he pulled a tissue from the box on her dresser and returned to the bed. "She's a very interesting person."

"Isn't she?" Melinda plucked the tissue from his fingers and blew her nose. "She had so many stories about the art of conjure and the Oracles of Santeria." She sniffed.

"Honey, I know you like Tilly, but I think it's best we leave the voodoo to her." He stuffed the doll into his pants pocket. "I'll hold on to this if you don't mind."

Melinda stood and slipped her arms around his waist. "Okay, Daddy." She looked up and smiled. Frank felt protective as he gazed at her face so innocent and childlike.

"I love you, Daddy."

"I love you, too, darlin'." Frank stroked her hair and

patted her shoulders.

He smiled at Melinda then stepped back and turned to link his arm in Joan's to lead her out of the room.

"You handled that very well," Joan said after closing Melinda's door. "I think you should be the official spokesman from now on."

Frank put on a startled look. "I don't know if I want to sign up for permanent spokes duty."

Joan giggled and squeezed his arm. "What did the insurance agent say about Rex's law suit?"

Frank smiled sardonically. "It seems our policy doesn't cover accidents of this type, but he did suggest increasing our coverage, lowering our deductible and paying a higher premium."

"No wonder they're so rich." Joan shook her head. "What are you going to do with that thing?" She pointed to his pocket.

"I'm going to let Gene take care of it. He knows just the place to bury it."

# Chapter Eighteen

Frank tapped on the side of the aquarium and smiled. "Good morning my little cold-blooded natatory creatures." He sprinkled food across the top of the water and then shuffled into the kitchen. He flicked on the light and rubbed his eyes. His jaw cracking yawn was accompanied by a loud hum as he scratched his fingernails across his ribs.

Blackie slinked around Frank's slippers and rubbed up against his legs as he meowed. He had unenthusiastically become a member of the family by a vote of five to one. Of course with Joan casting the opposing vote, Blackie had lovingly adopted her as his preferred human.

"I know," Frank said. "You want your breakfast." He opened the pantry and checked the shelf. "Tuna, tuna, tuna," he said running a finger down the cans. "How do you feel about tuna?"

Blackie meowed.

"Tuna it is." Frank positioned the opener on the side of the can. Blackie yowled louder at hearing it.

"All right, keep your boots on."

Frank set the dish on the floor and stopped to listen. He thought he heard the front door open. He tapped the fork on the edge of the dish as Blackie nosed his way past it.

"Hi."

Frank jumped and flipped tuna meat across the floor as he looked up. "Man! You scared me!"

"Sorry," Gene said.

"Where have you been? I asked you to bury that voodoo doll days ago, and you never came back. I was beginning to think you met with foul play." Frank snagged a rag and wiped the floor in several places. "I would have called the police but you're such a vagabond, I figured you just got a wild hair and went back home for awhile."

Gene grinned and tilted his head. "Nope, didn't go home, but you'll never guess who I ran into at the crossroads."

Frank looked up from his kneeling position, one eyebrow rose in query. "Who?"

Gene held up an index finger. "Don't go away," he said and rushed to the front door. He returned a moment later.

"Helen!" Frank said and stepped toward her to give her a hug.

"It's been a long time, Frank."

"How did you know where to find Gene?" he asked.

Helen placed an index finger to her temple and rolled her eyes. "It could have been the note he left on the kitchen table that said...*Gone to Franks for an indeterminate amount of time*." She laughed. "I can't believe he actually thought I ran off with a salesman," she challenged softly. "I distinctly remember telling him I was going to visit my mother."

Gene blushed. "I must have been preoccupied."

"You must have been drunk," she corrected. "It was a coincidence that I got lost on the way here and found him burying something on the side of the road."

"A coincidence?" Frank looked at Gene.

Gene shrugged. "I'm kind of getting used to them."

"You never told me what you were doing out there," Joan said curiously.

"Good Morning," Joan said from the kitchen door. "Helen is that you?" She smiled. "I hardly recognized you with blond hair."

"Bless your heart," Helen said as she gave Joan a hug. "You're the only one who's noticed."

Gene and Frank looked at each other.

"I love it," Joan said fluffing the shoulder length ends. "I wonder how I would look as a blond."

Helen ran her fingers through her hair and grinned. "I thought; if I've only one life to live, let me live it as a blond."

Joan smiled. "Pancakes anyone?" she asked as she opened the cupboard and pulled out a brown plastic bowl.

"Hey, isn't that our popcorn bowl?" Frank asked.

Joan shrugged. "Pancake batter won't hurt it."

Frank reached into a cupboard and pulled out a glass bowl. "Maybe not, but I don't feel like popcorn flavored pancakes this morning."

Joan stuck her tongue out at him as he turned away. "What ever you say dear," she mocked.

A loud engine started up next door. Joan tipped her head back and groaned.

"What's that?" Gene asked.

Frank walked to the window, stood on his toes and strained to look out. "It's a backhoe. Robert's is digging a swimming pool in his back yard."

"When are *we* getting a swimming pool?" Joan asked.

"I'm still working on my *first* million," Frank said in the most reasonable tone he could muster. "Maybe we can have one in about ten years."

Joan turned to look at him. "You mean I have to listen to them splashing around in their built in swimming pool for ten years before I get one of my own?"

"I'll buy you some ear plugs," Frank said with a humorless smile.

"Guess what?" Helen said as she stirred the batter while Joan added eggs. "Gene found a job nearby so we will be moving close to you in a couple of weeks. Isn't that great?"

"You got a job buddy?" Frank asked. "Doing what?"

Gene gave him a shamefaced glance. "I had Tilly's rash treatment oil analyzed by a local laboratory. They broke it down, and there doesn't seem to be a patent on it so I found a partner willing to produce the first batch."

Frank's mouth dropped open. "You're stealing Tilly's remedy?"

"It's not really stealing," Gene argued. "It's just a recipe that is free to anyone who wants to do something with it. You know me, a true humanitarian, I just like helping people." His eyebrows flew up. "Hey! You could write an ad jingle for it!"

Frank stared at him. "Who's your partner?"

Gene dipped his head and smiled. "Rex Roberts."

The doorbell rang. Frank said, "We've got to talk about this," as he pointed an index finger at Gene on his way to the door.

"Hello Mr. Beal," Bobby MacCormack shoved his hand at Frank through the open door.

Frank shook it. "Hello Bobby, what brings you here so early?"

"My family is taking my aunt and uncle to the airport, and I thought Mel would like to come along."

Frank opened the door wider. "Come in." He looked up the stairs. "Melinda! Someone is here to see you."

Melinda appeared at the top of the stairs and looked down. She screamed, wrapped her robe tightly around her middle and backed out of sight. "Daddy, why didn't you say it was Bobby?" Her voice came out in a wispy croak. "I'm not even dressed yet."

Frank shrugged. "It's Bobby."

"I'm getting dressed. I'll be down in a minute."

"You might as well come in and relax," Frank said sounding amused. "This may take awhile. You eat yet?"

The kitchen smelled of blueberry pancakes, bacon, scrambled eggs and fresh coffee. "Bobby's here to take Melinda to the airport," Frank announced.

"And where are you off to?" Joan asked suspiciously.

Bobby smiled. "My parents and I are seeing my aunt and uncle off. They've been visiting from Brazil."

"Bobby's aunt Tilly is married to Tito Tortuga," Frank said with a shrewd wink.

"What?!" Gene exclaimed. "Tilly's your aunt?"

"My mom's sister." Bobby nodded and took a step back.

"The one that makes rash oil?" Gene sounded like an interrogating officer. "That's good for cat scratches and bad gums?"

Bobby smiled. "Among other things. She's an herbalist and has spared a lot of people from unnecessary surgery."

"What about your uncle? He's a gardener isn't he?" Frank asked.

"He has a lot of side jobs," Bobby said as he took the glass of orange juice Joan offered him. "Thanks." He sipped, licked his lips and sipped again. "He cooks, grows exotic plants and practices the art of conjure. I've always known him as a priest of Santeria."

"Where is that?"

Bobby laughed. "It's not where, it's what. Santeria is a religion," he explained. "Uncle Tito only works for the fun of it. He's very rich. Orishas and guardian spirits predict numbers that will come out in the lottery or what horse will win a race but Tito is the only one who can interpret the coded clues, and he does it regularly."

"Where can I get one of these Orishas?" Gene asked.

Bobby raised a resistant hand. "You don't want to get one, believe me. Don't even mess with the stuff. You can cause yourself a lot of trouble."

"I believe you." Gene smiled.

"I'm sorry Bobby," Joan interrupted. "You haven't met Melinda's aunt Helen," she said as she poured a cup of coffee.

Helen waved a batter covered spoon. "Hi."

Bobby smiled. "The pleasure is mine."

Joan handed the coffee to Frank and stretched to whisper in his ear, "His manners have improved since his last visit."

Frank whispered, "Remarkably."

"Have a seat Bobby," Frank motioned toward the dining room table, "and tell me more about your family."

Bobby sat in one of the chairs facing the back yard. "There's not much to tell. My mom calls her sister when she's worried about someone in the family. Aunt Tilly and Uncle Tito come and straighten it out. This time it was me she was worried about."

"You?" Frank's brow knitted.

The corners of Bobby's lips tipped up in a crooked smile. "Yeah, my parents want me to go to college in the fall. I didn't see the advantage in it, as you know." He shrugged. "Aunt Tilly and Uncle Tito came and set me straight. I'm going to Berkley in the fall."

Frank grinned and nodded his approval. "A mind is a terrible thing to waste." He imagined Tilly and Tito standing over a boiling cauldron stirring in chicken heads, snail shells, John and Valerain root, fly's legs then sprinkling it all with the dust from a moth's wings. "And just how did they set you straight?" he asked adding half and half to his coffee. He lifted it and took a cautious sip. "Did they use some kind of magic spell on you?"

"No," Bobby chuckled. "They never use magic on family." He gave Frank a pensive look. "I think it was something Aunt Tilly said."

"What was that?"

"She said going through life without an education was like trying to play ping pong in the dark."

Frank smiled in contemplation then sipped at his coffee.

Melinda tip toed up behind Bobby and placed her hands over his eyes.

He smiled. "Hey Mel."

"How did you know it was me?" she giggled and sat down beside him.

"I smelled the baby powder." He turned and laughed.

Frank gazed up at her lovingly. No wonder he had such a hard time accepting that she was growing up, she hadn't outgrown baby powder yet.

"I use it on my hair when I don't have time to wash it," she announced crinkling her nose.

Joan walked in with a stack of plates. "Don't get too comfortable young lady; I need you to set the table."

Helen followed with the plate of bacon and scrambled eggs. Gene brought in a couple of extra chairs, and Matt tagged after him carrying a kitchen stool.

"Is everyone here?" Joan asked as she placed a steaming platter of pancakes in the center of the table.

She looked around. "Where's Susan?"

"She's next door watching them dig the pool for Mr. Roberts," Matt said as he picked up two pancakes with his fingers and flopped them on his plate.

"Go and tell her breakfast is ready," Joan said. "And wash those filthy hands Mister."

Matt sighed deeply and reluctantly slid from the stool. "Make me a happy face, okay mom?" He ran to the front door.

"Okay, honey," Joan said. "And don't slam the…"

She didn't finish her sentence before the front door slammed behind him.

"What's a happy face?" Helen asked.

"It's this!" Gene said and displayed a huge smile.

"I'm so happy you're wearing your teeth," Helen said and kissed his cheek.

Joan arranged Matt's pancakes in a stack. "This is a happy face," she explained. She put scrambled eggs at the top of his plate to represent hair. She curved a mouth with a strip of bacon and carefully placed two blueberries on each side to indicate eyes.

"Oh how cute." Helen said.

"How come you never do that for me?" Frank asked teasingly.

Joan grinned. "One happy face at a time please."

"Aunt Helen," Melinda blinked. "When did you get here?"

Helen flashed Melinda a smile. "It looks like I arrived just in time to enjoy this wonderful breakfast."

Matt burst through the door, ran to the table and hopped up on the stool. "She's coming."

"Did you wash your hands?" Joan asked.

Matt nodded. He bent over with his face just inches from his plate. He grabbed his fork and began eating as if he expected the food to run away. "I washed them with the hose," he said between chews.

"Pass the butter please," Gene said.

Helen said, "Joan, this is the best maple syrup I ever had."

"Daddy, is it okay if I go to Berkley on week-ends to visit Bobby when he's in college?"

Frank gave Melinda a bright smile. "If your mother and I can go, too."

"Oh, Daddy," she pouted.

Susan came through the door with a smile and a hum. She was armored up in her hard hat and work boots with her clipboard under her arm.

# Chapter Nineteen

A wedge of morning sunlight fell across Frank's Sherman Clay upright piano. He lightly tapped the keys with the tips of his fingers patiently waiting for inspiration to ignite.

Matt appeared beside him. "Morning dad."

"Morning Matt, ready for school?"

Matt nodded and smiled with a soap cleaned freckled face.

"Knock, knock," Matt said squirming with anticipation.

Frank slipped an arm around Matt's shoulders. "Who's there?"

"Banana."

"Banana who?" Frank played along.

"Knock, knock," Matt said excitedly.

Frank's brows knitted, and he flashed an uncertain smile.

"Who's there?"

"Banana," Matt said again.

"Banana who?"

"Knock, knock," Matt repeated.

"Come on, aren't you gonna tell me who's there?"

"Orange," Matt chirped.

"Orange who?"

"Orange you glad I didn't say banana again?" Matt slapped his hands over his mouth. His eyes turned to slits, and his shoulders jiggled with laughter.

Frank smiled and patted Matt's back. "You got me."

"Matt, go tell Susan the car will be leaving in five minutes," Joan said as she pulled on her jacket.

"Why do I always have to go get Susan?"

"To avoid getting yelled at," Joan explained.

Matt's shoulders slumped.

Frank gently squeezed the back of Matt's neck. "Go ahead buddy, it's because you're the fastest."

Matt looked up. He flashed a mischievous smile and ran toward the stairs.

"Now why can't I think of things like that?" Joan asked.

Frank shrugged. "We can't all be ingenious when it comes to motivating people."

Joan walked over and opened the drapes across the window that overlooked the side of the house. "How can you work when it's so dark in here?"

Frank winced back the sunlight. "A beautiful day distracts me from my work. I actually use it as a reward. Once I've accomplished what I set out to do, I allow myself to enjoy..." his words were cut short when he spotted the black satin and lace bustier corset hanging on the clothes line. "I allow myself to enjoy..."

"Enjoy what?" Joan asked with a seductive smile. She began to walk towards him with her heavy lidded eyes gliding from his face to his chest and resting just south of the border.

Frank felt his jaw clench. Although Tilly had

removed the perfection from the family to his satisfaction. This obsession Joan had with her corset lingered. Her episodes were less frequent, and the intensity had diminished somewhat, still he struggled with finding a healthy balance of sex, family, work and recreation in their marriage. In precisely that order.

Frank blinked back the glare. "What's that on the clothes line hanging along side your black lingerie?"

Joan stopped and turned to look. "Tea bags and paper towels."

Frank frowned. "Why are you hanging tea bags on the clothes line?"

"I'm saving money, they can be re-used," she explained. "If you think I'm going to wait ten years to have a swimming pool you're out of your mind."

Frank sighed. "Do we have to continue to compete with the Robert's?"

"Oh sure, easy for you to say. You don't have to listen to Joan prattle on about all the things Rex is buying for her," she complained. "Jewelry, vacations, a swimming pool..."

Frank raised a hand. "The Robert's don't have three children either."

"Good morning," Susan said. "Daddy, one of the light bulbs in the bathroom is out, and the water doesn't drain fast enough in the shower. It's a health hazard."

"I'll get right on that," Frank said as he jotted it on an imaginary list.

"Okay, go ahead and joke..." Susan said as she set her clipboard down to put on her jacket. "...but don't blame me when someone comes down with planter's warts or athlete's foot."

"Honey, you'd be the last one I'd blame."

"So, I've been thinking Frank," Joan said. "If I can save on household expenses and work full-time instead of part-time, do you think we could have a pool in two years?"

Frank frowned. "I'm not sure it's a good idea for you to work full time. Who will pick the kids up from school? Do the grocery shopping? Cooking?"

"You, of course."

Frank's face pinched into a look of protest. "Just because I'm home doesn't mean I'm not working."

"We can't have a pool," Susan announced. "At least not a built-in pool."

"What?" Joan and Frank said in unison. "Why?"

Susan rolled her eyes. "According to the rules and regulations for swimming pool permits your backyard has to be at least thirty-nine point thirty-seven feet wide."

"So?" Frank said.

"So, ours is only thirty-six."

"How do you know that?" Joan asked.

"I measured it."

Joan blinked. "I mean how do you know about the rules and regulations for swimming pools."

Susan shrugged. "I looked it up at the library."

Joan and Frank exchanged a surprised glance.

"Mr. Robert's yard isn't big enough for a pool either," Susan said matter of factly. "I measured his yard, too. It's a half foot smaller than ours."

"Then how did he get his permit?" Frank asked.

Susan shrugged again. "He must have lied."

A slow smile spread across Frank's face. A feeling of joy bubbled up and puffed out his chest. He was a bit light headed, intoxicated with a kind of lofty delight. The relentless pursuit of stuff, and how much was enough had suddenly been revealed to him. In a single moment of clarity he was able to clearly view a defect that was far from charming. The unconquerable but ludicrous grip of rivalry had been exposed, and he realized now it was time to let it go.

"When I told him what I found at the library, he had a real funny look on his face," Susan said.

Frank laughed out loud. "I'll bet he did." Then he became serious. "Did you threaten to report him?"

Susan rolled her eyes more dramatically this time. "I'm not stupid. I want to swim in it."

"Mom," Melinda said. "Let's go. Mr. Moore said if I'm late for my English class one more time I'll get a Saturday of detention. You don't want that hanging over your head do you?" She smoothed her hands down the leather vest Bobby had given her.

Joan placed a hand over her heart. "Heaven's no, you would miss a day without Bobby in Saturday detention." She smiled and kissed Frank on the lips. "Have a good day."

Matt appeared next to Frank. "I hope you write another neat song like the one for the shoe polish. Lickity spit." He gave Frank two thumbs up.

"Just for you, buddy." Frank gave Matt a hug and without any premeditation said, "What do you think about going over to the animal shelter after school and picking out a dog?"

Matt's eyes grew round, and his mouth dropped open. "Neato! Thanks dad!"

Joan finally got the kids herded out, and the house fell silent except for the notes Frank plunked.

"*I've got you under my skin,*" he sang then shook his head. The advertisement had to speak of healing, not affliction.

He tried another. "*Cuddle up a little closer, I'm rash free.*"

Gene had insisted that Frank's company handle all the advertising for Tilly's oil that had been thoughtfully named, Santeria healing oil. Of course, Gene and Rex made Tilly a partner when the first batch of oil failed to perform. She supplied the missing ingredients, which turned out to be an undisclosed ratio of Valerian root and pomegranate tonic accompanied by a rhyming chant. Frank didn't completely pass on this ground floor opportunity; he invested half their savings in Santeria healing oil and was just waiting for the right moment to tell Joan.

His eyes brightened. "*At last, my rash has gone away, my itching days are over, and I can sing a song.*" He laughed. Etta James wouldn't be happy about that. Besides, the oil was a lot more than just a rash remedy.

The doorbell rang.

Frank opened the door. It was Rex Roberts. His smile was humble, a flickering expression seldom seen on his customarily arrogant face. He shifted his feet with an uncomfortable looking posture.

"Hello Frank."

"Rex. What can I do for you?"

"Yes, well." his eyes wandered toward the flower beds and across the lawn. "I just wanted you to know that I have been released by my doctor, and I have dismissed the personal injury law suit."

"Really?" Frank had to work to extinguish the look of surprise.

"Yes, Gene explained that he was the one who was responsible for the mishap." Rex put a hand on the small of his back. "And that oil that Tilly makes seems to have cured any injury that resulted in my fall."

"That's good news." Frank smiled.

"Hey, and I'm real glad you'll be writing the jingle for the oil. I know it will be great." Rex shoved his hands deep into his pockets and looked down at his shoes.

"You want to come in for some coffee?" Frank asked.

Rex's head jerked up. "No thanks, I have to get back to supervise the pool builders."

Frank smiled. "Yes, your new *built-in* pool. Congratulations."

Rex dipped his head in obvious embarrassment. "Yes, well." He turned to leave then turned back. "I hope you and your family will feel free to come over and use the pool."

"Yeah?" Frank nodded his head.

"Sure, anytime."

"Thanks."

Rex cleared his throat. "I also have a new gardener. I'm sure he would have the time to mow your yard while he's here. I'm happy to tag it on to my bill."

"Well, that's very neighborly of you Rex. Thanks."

"No problem."

Frank watched him walk down the walkway and turn towards his house before closing the door. Frank grinned. Susan rides again. Her naive techniques were more valuable than any voodoo spell on the market.

He tapped lightly on the aquarium and watched the fish swim lazily from one side of the glass to the next. Must be nice to float around aimlessly all day. He thought about summer and looked forward to taking quiet dips in Robert's pool when everyone was off doing their summer things.

He sat back down at his piano and smiled. He was still taken aback by Robert's dropping the lawsuit. The family had been tested by a sea of mysterious mishaps except weird and wonderful miracles appeared and embraced them to return them physically and mentally safe and emotionally wiser bobbing to the surface every time. Another miracle, their lives were full of them.

Printed in the United States
46922LVS00001B/130-141

9 780977 010769